Where Legends Ride

The hanging judge was ready and eager to swing Cassidy, Waco and Pike high from his Colorado gallows until it was suddenly discovered that they were, in fact, innocent. This was bad news for the bloodthirsty old judge and a stern warning for the three young hell-raisers to mend their ways. So they rode south, bought up a piece of land and settled down to honest work and the quiet life.

But Buffalo County was not what it seemed and soon the trio found themselves drawn into a raging blood-feud involving an arrogant cattle king, a bunch of jail-birds and a lethal young drifter on the run from the law. Now Cassidy, Waco and Pike must buckle on their guns to fight for survival.

Colorado might have been bloody but Buffalo County was worse!

Where Legends Ride

PAUL WHEELAHAN

A Black Horse Western

ROBERT HALE · LONDON

© Paul Wheelahan 2001
First published in Great Britain 2001

ISBN 0 7090 6862 X

Robert Hale Limited
Clerkenwell House
Clerkenwell Green
London EC1R 0HT

Typeset by
Derek Doyle & Associates, Liverpool.
Printed and bound in Great Britain by
Antony Rowe Limited, Wiltshire

1

Hellions' Playground

Jubal Creech lay asleep in a patch of moonlight with the black muzzle of a Colt .45 two inches from his face. He was sprawled on his back with legs and arms outstretched, his unshaven jaw showing blue-black and his barrel chest rising and falling evenly to the rhythm of his breathing. He stank of rye whiskey and some trick of the moonlight made it seem he was smiling to himself.

He should see it coming, Hanline thought venomously as his finger tightened on the trigger. Shouldn't just be lying there likely dreaming about how he gypped me on them mustangs then got off with her . . . when it comes. He should know he's gonna die. . . .

The badman's slitted eyes cut sideways at the lush shape of his ex-mistress sleeping gracefully on her side in the shadowy half of the rumpled bed, her back to her new-old lover, blissfully unaware of the presence of sudden death in the derelict Running M's big front room.

'Double-dealin' jade!' breathed the badman, and extended his gun arm until the muzzle almost brushed

Creech's brow. He was a man who had killed before, was never more ready to do so again than in this hushed midnight hour in the foothills. Someone he'd almost trusted had gypped him out of a thousand dollars' worth of horseflesh, then run off with his woman. Nobody ever had a better motive to kill. 'So long, shyster!' he hissed through his teeth, and was silently thumbing the hammer back when the abrupt howling of a wolf almost caused him to drop the gun. He backed away from the bed, fearful his dangerous victim must wake.

Young Luke Pike likely had stronger nerves and a clearer conscience than Skar Hanline. Even so he too was startled by that eerie feral cry which came tumbling down from the higher slopes, catching all three horsemen exposed under the full blaze of moonlight flooding the lower pasture a rifle-shot below the outlaw hideout.

'Cut it!' he hissed as his bony, rat-tailed dun began acting up. 'And that goes double for you too, Ugly. Don't you start up either!'

The big yellow dog's hackles remained quiveringly erect. But it didn't bark even though every primitive instinct clamored to give tongue.

The lithe rider hipped around in his saddle to see how his partners were reacting. Waco looked uneasy, as well he might, for the three were trespassing with unlawful intent upon the turf of one of the most notorious figures in the county here. If that old timber-wolf should alert Creech and whoever else was with him up there, then whatever slight advantage they might have had would be gone.

Both looked a question at Cassidy who said nothing as he lifted his gaze to the crumbling ranch house atop the rise, yet his firm nod was unmistakable. It meant he intended to go through with it no matter what; get up there and finish what they'd come to do, namely confront Jubal Creech and collect what they were rightly owed.

Sounded simple if you said it fast, which was exactly what they'd done back in town. But it seemed a far riskier notion out here in enemy territory with a baleful moon turning night into day and that timber-wolf continuing to howl like he would wake the dead.

The manner in which Clem Waco and Luke Pike just shrugged and swung in alongside Abe Cassidy's crumple-eared chestnut to begin the ascent, said more about their partnership and character than had been contained in a recent flattering piece about them in the *County Express*.

They were different in most ways that signified, these three, even in a time and place where characters abounded and the violent change and challenge of a new country opening up made the unusual an everyday reality.

The young riders who came and went in these wild borderlands as free as the prairie winds on their runty mustangs were most likely to be sighted going to or coming from one reckless kind of money-making enter-prise or another, or perhaps just drowsing their fiddle-footed way along some remote trail or another, maybe stopping by an old soddy, cattle-spread or one-horse town for an hour or a month acting like they believed the sunny days would never end and they'd be free and footloose forever.

They would take on just about anything; horse-breaking on the big spreads or maybe herding stock to the new rail-heads in the south. They were not above day laboring if the wages were okay, and particularly if the boss man had a pretty daughter or three as an added bonus.

Sometimes they gambled for serious money in tough dives along the Cimarron or Cow Creek. They hired out as trail guides, had scouted for the Army on occasion, even dug deep and unsuccessfully for gold in the crab-apple hills southwest of Flint City. For fun of the outdoor kind, what they liked best of all was to hunt. They had a taste for difficult game, the more dangerous the better: bobcats, mountain lions, bighorn sheep, big brown bears up in the Rockies foothills or buffalo out on the wide plains.

What all this boiled down to was three Tennessee-born youngsters living out their childhood fantasies of life in the Golden West, and living them to the hilt.

The Creech job had seemed simple enough to men temporarily out of work. Herd twenty head of fresh-broken broncos from Sweetwater to Harrison's Bend for a generous fee, a quarter down and the rest on completion. Simplicity itself.

Only thing, by the time they returned to Sweetwater, the drive successfully completed, it was to find that Creech had disappeared following a ruckus involving badman Skar Hanline and a woman of mutual acquaintance named Rebecca.

'Nothing we can do for you until we get a line on where those hardnoses were headed, and whether or not Creech mightn't have quit the county altogether with what he owes you and some others he gypped, boys,' was how the lugubrious sheriff of Sweetwater responded to their demand for assistance. 'So just you leave it to the law. It might be slow and creaky at times but it always gets there in the end.'

The hell with that!

Tracking critters or people was their specialty, as they'd proved yet again tonight when the faintest remnant of skil-fully blotted sign, identified as that of Creech and the woman, led them to this derelict spread in the foothills.

Where that lonesome wolf-song had finally faded by the time they had gained the plateau, where they paused in back of the barn to study the house and confer in sign language how they would go about it.

Three doors, three of them. What could be simpler?

And still no thunderblast of murderous gunfire from behind that front window which reflected the moon like liquid gold.

But Skar Hanline had managed to gear himself up again after spending five cold-sweating minutes with one foot out the bedroom door, terrified Creech would awaken. But the howling of a timber-wolf was as familiar as the whiff of hard-tack coffee to both outdoorsman Jubal Creech and his two sidekicks out in the shotgun bunkhouse. All three slept though it like innocents. Creech was now dreaming he was the cattleman king of Colorado and running for Congress with Rebecca at last his blushing bride – as death again cat-footed across moon-silvered floorboards to reach the bed-end.

But the woman wasn't sleeping any longer, hadn't been ever since the wolf began. Voluptuous Rebecca Dulane was Springfield's unchallenged beauty queen, a tempestuous woman with fiery ways and an uneasy conscience who had every good reason to sleep as light as a falling snowflake. She was never more wide awake than at that moment when something long and lean passed between herself and the window standing wide open to the night.

A bare sixty feet distant outside, three stealthy figures were ghosting across the new spring grass when a flung leather cushion struck Skar Hanline in the back of the head causing him to involuntarily jerk trigger and pump a .44 slug harmlessly into the pillow by Jubal Creech's ear which brought the badman exploding upwards and clawing for the double gunrig looped over the bedhead.

It went swiftly from there as the head-jolting blast of the shot awoke every man, horse and wild critter within a wide radius of the house on the plateau.

From the smoke-choked bedroom where the moon-wash still flooded in, came a woman's piercing screams, the crash of warring six-guns snarling like savage dogs in a confined space, the ominous thud of a falling body. Outside in the yard, three intruders were backing up defensively as Creech's half-awake henchmen stumbled into sight from the bunkhouse away to their right. Reacting to the eruption of violence from the house, the hardcase pair sighted gun-toting strangers in the moon-light and promptly opened up.

'Cover!' Cassidy bawled, and sheer youthful agility saw all three dive to safety in back of the heavy log water-trough before the shooters could get their eye in. With wood splinters flying and geysers of bullet-lifted water drenching them, the partners were no longer thinking of justice, fair play or even getting square as they hunkered down tight. By nature they enjoyed a good ruckus, but plainly this was far too risky for their blood.

The gunmen stormed right on by to vanish into the house. Three sodden heads raised warily. Although no longer under direct fire, there was no way they were going to get involved in the total confusion and gun-chaos grip-ping the ranch house, with shooting and shouting figures rushing to and from house and horseyards beneath a canopy of drifting gunsmoke for what seemed an eternity.

They'd come to square accounts with Creech, but were unable to identify his powerful figure amongst those shad-owy figures charging about through a haze of gunsmoke.

So they waited.

It only seemed a long wait. Barely a violent minute elapsed before the sudden stutter of racing hoofbeats arose from the yard on the far side of the house, beating away for the high country. From somewhere the woman screamed again. A .45 exploded and gunflashes flared wickedly as the blurring outlines of dark riders broke away from the black moonshadows of bunkhouse and corral to give chase, howling and cussing like muleskinners as they lashed their mounts upslope into the brooding timber-line.

Luke Pike was first to rise cautiously. When his long figure failed to attract hot lead, Waco and Cassidy deemed it safe to follow suit. By this time the horsemen were gone and all was suddenly skeleton-still on this hazy plateau beneath the whitecapped titan of Emerald Peak.

'Let's dust.' Waco sounded hoarse.

Cassidy was tempted, but Pike shook his head.

'Wouldn't be right,' he said in his slow, country-boy way. He nodded at the ranch house which now boasted bullet-shattered front windows. 'Could be someone hurt in there.'

Waco and Cassidy traded looks. They knew he was right. And they had their ethics, difficult to find though they could be at times. The ethic of maybe leaving someone to die, friend or foe, was one they weren't prepared to defy, even if entering that house right now might seem about as smart as sticking your arm down a rattler's hole to see if it was occupied.

They need not have worried.

There was nobody left alive within the cordite-choked ranch house. Nobody at all but the bullet-riddled body of Jubal Creech sprawled across a wildly disarrayed bed, arms outflung and lock-jawed face turned starkly to the moon.

It seemed to take a long, heavy-footed time to get out of the house and make their way back down to the pine-fringed pasture. Although no strangers to the rougher side of life, Cassidy, Waco and Pike had somehow always managed to avoid any situation which bridged the gap between high-spirited hell-raising and sudden death. Until tonight, that was.

Sure, they'd admittedly had it in for Creech and had publicly vowed to hunt him down and get what they were owed, one way or another. But that didn't mean they'd wanted him dead.

They didn't talk; the stark image of Creech was too vivid in their minds for that. They'd decide what was to be done after they were mounted and on their way back to town. As they approached the stand of black jackpines where they'd hidden the horses, Waco whistled his muddy-colored roan, wondered vaguely why it didn't answer or appear. Yet he was in no way concerned until Goober suddenly appeared and growled a warning, by which time it was too late. Sharp movement erupted in the heavy shadow of the trees and a familiar figure with a long-barrelled pistol in hand stepped into view, yellow light striking fire from the star pinned to his chest.

'Hands up!' barked the sheriff of Sweetwater. 'Looks to me like you boys should've took my advice and left me to handle this.' He jerked his head upslope. 'We headed out just as soon as I got a tip Creech was holing up here. Sure hope no harm's befallen that feller, yessir I surely do.'

The rawboned peace officer with the handlebar mustaches sounded calm and almost paternal. He was far less benign some fifteen minutes later when, having searched the Running M headquarters, examined the corpse and listened carefully to their account of events, he sternly ordered Abe 'Friendly' Cassidy, Luke Pike and Clem Waco clapped in manacles and advised against their saying anything further until they had secured an attorney. A good one.

In Sweetwater, the charge was murder. The partners protested it had to be a joke, but nobody was laughing.

A single overhead lamp lighted the jailhouse. Head in his hands, Luke Pike stared at its reflection in the water bucket, shivering as the cold from the floor crept into his boots.

He jumped as a none too gentle fist thudded against his shoulder.

'What the hell . . .' he protested.

'You're broodin', you Raccoon Creek chicken-liver,' Waco accused. 'Go on, deny you're sittin' here frettin' about tomorrow and what these hicks might do to us.'

'The hell I was!'

Waco sat beside him and threw an arm about his shoulders. 'Look at it this way. We've got ourselves a good attorney, we're gettin' the best judge in the county comin' in, everybody in town's backin' us . . . and most important, we're innocent. So we're home free. Right, Cass?'

Sitting up on his narrow bunk, Cassidy nodded. 'Sure, the man is right. But you didn't mention the most important thing, Clem. We're fighting this thing together, so there's no way we can lose . . . not here in the West . . . so let's hear it.'

Together they crooned:

'Into the West where the sun never sets
Into the life that's as good as it gets.'

13

They broke up, laughing. Washing up in back, the sheriff heard every word, was shaking his head and grinning as he came through, heading for his desk. He'd always liked the Kentucky boys, and genuinely regretted their present fix.

But like them, he shared their optimism and was looking forward to a quick trial and early acquittal, when he noticed the postal clerk had left a letter on his desk.

He frowned when he saw it was from the 23rd. District Court, Ratenal County, Colorado. He ripped it open, paled. It was a wire stating that the circuit judge had been taken ill, and his replacement would be Judge Moran.

The lawman slumped back in his swivel chair, looking like he'd aged a decade. Moran was otherwise known as the Hanging Judge. He couldn't meet the prisoners' eyes.

They didn't do things by halves in this corner of the territory. The hangman arrived in town aboard the judge's coach, and next morning, trial day, was to be heard explaining his apparatus to the goggle-eyed bystanders clustered round his portable gallows as towners continued to stream up to the clapboard courthouse in numbers.

'The length of the drop is the height of the condemned plus twelve inches leeway. The tallest of the three I measured up, Pike, is six two, so the distance from crossbeam to ground will be seven feet two inches.' He patted his bulging weskit. 'No chance of error when I'm runnin' the show, folks.'

His words carried clearly into Judge Moran's chambers at the rear of the courthouse where that worthy stood shrugging into his musty black robes of office. The judge's ethics were in no way compromised either by the hangman's arrival ahead of a verdict – and aboard his private

14

coach – any more than they were by this blatant presumption of guilt. A hanging judge in the truest sense of the term, he would in truth much prefer to be listening to the executioner enlightening the rubes outside than to what the sheriff was saying to him.

'I fear now I may have been over-hasty in preferring murder charges, your honor. In light of subsequent investigations and due consideration, that is. Circumstantial evidence might well have initially suggested the accused had done Creech in. But now we're certain there was another man involved and that this was almost certainly Skar Hanline, a man with a record, a violent temper and a blood grudge to settle with the dead man. I fail to see how this case can properly proceed until Hanline or the woman involved are located. Don't you agree?'

'Don't go wishy-washy on me, Sheriff.' The judge was an iron-gray man with sunken black eyes that blazed out from the ambush of wild and bushy brows. His cape went over a tightly buttoned frock-coat which was worn both winter and summer. He angled his gnarled head to peer through a spyhole affording a view of the courtroom, snorted when he sighted the tall figure in stylish gray-silk suit and four-in-hand tie.

'Buffington, the outlaw-loving swine!' He turned sharply. 'How do three bums get to afford the Capital's highest-priced defence attorney, Sheriff? Riddle me that.'

'Seems those hard working boys have been saving up for a rainy day, so I discovered. Got over a thousand salted away in the Federal Bank, so they have. When I asked what they'd planned to do with it, they said maybe buy up a piece of land and go ranching someday.'

'You didn't swallow that?'

The lawman shrugged. He was an unflappable peace

officer with an impressive reputation. But since the killing and the arrests he hadn't slept well.

'My subsequent investigations at the death site tended to support the accused's testimony that three other men and a woman were actively involved in Creech's death. I am convinced one of those men was Skar Hanline, a two-gun desperado with powerful motives to kill Creech.'

'Unsupported statements by desperate felons cut no ice with me, Mr Lawman.' The judge started a little at a sudden upsurge in the noise level coming from the over-flowing courtroom. 'What the devil. . . !' He again jammed an eye to the spyhole to see three confident-looking young men in manacles being escorted through the main door by the deputies to an outburst of spontaneous applause from the tight-packed crowd.

They looked more like boys than men!

That was the judge's first reaction. He'd expected to find the accused much older, evil-looking specimens. Not that it affected his attitude to the case in hand, however. The contrary, rather. He hated lawbreakers as a breed but detested the young as a class. As terminal cancer white-anted his bitter insides the old man's hatreds spread wider and deeper.

'Damnation! What's the meaning of this public exhibition, Sheriff?'

'Well, I'm afraid Waco, Cassidy and Pike are pretty popular youngsters hereabouts, Your Honor. Only new-come to this corner of the Territory, it's true, but just while I've had them locked up these Kentuckians seem to have made friends all over, especially amongst the young women of the town—'

'Enough, blast you! One of the prime things I've been campaigning against for years is this tendency to idolize

16

scum and whitewash the blackest villains, a development which you obviously support, sir.'

'But—'

'Lead the way, sir!' The judge was flushed and heated-looking, an alarming combination of funereal black garb and hectic red complexion. 'We shall see how fine they look when they are hanging off a gibbet-pole by high noon!'

The trial, in Sweetwater, of The People *vs* Abel Cassidy, Lucas Pike and Clement Waco drew a large crowd and was a farce from beginning to end.

It began with a ringing condemnation of the accused 'and their verminous class' from the bench, and seemed certain to end some four hours later with the defence attorney long silenced by Moran's hostility, and the hanging judge instructing the jury, not on whether it should find the accused guilty, but on their legal and moral obligation to do so, and fast.

Then it happened. At first the dazed men in the dock were but dimly aware of the sudden rising clamor around them until the incessant banging of the gavel and the sheer tumult enveloping the place dragged them back into the reality of a hot and sweating courtroom to find that its former order and solemnity had been replaced by a kind of communal frenzy.

People were gesticulating and shouting as they crowded to the windows, and the sheriff was nowhere to be seen. Red-faced and choleric, the judge gavelled his bench ferociously without it having the slightest effect.

Waco, Cassidy and Pike traded looks of bewilderment. Not hope. All hope had been buried by the judge's damning summation.

It seemed an eternity before sheriff and deputies were able to force their way through the congested lobby. When he finally emerged into the courthouse proper, looking flushed and triumphant, the lawman was clutching the bare arm of Rebecca Dulane, who in the cyclone eye of the upheaval, appeared as regal and imperious as some pagan warrior princess. Tossing her raven mane and with one hand on the butt of a holstered Colt, she cut flashing black eyes round the room to focus upon the outraged figure in black standing shaking behind his bench.

'What in the name of holy jurisprudence . . .' began the judge, but the sheriff's shout drowned him out and brought the uproar down to mere excited rumble all about him. The badgeman had the floor.

'Court business suspended, Judge Moran! I present before this assembly Miss Dulane, missing prime witness in the killing of Jubal Creech. She is surrendering herself into my custody on this day, along with the remains of Skar Hanline, whom she is prepared to swear was slain by herself and her kinsmen . . . also present . . .' Here he paused to indicate the trio of tall and rawboned strangers now ranged up protectively in back of their sister. 'Miss Dulane and her kinsmen will testify that Hanline pursued her with murderous intent the night he did wilfully slay, at Running M Ranch, Jubal Creech whom he accused of stealing her affections.'

He held a document and a walnut-butted Colt .45 pistol aloft.

'This here is a sworn deposition from Sheriff Miller of Dog City testifying that along with half his town he did witness Hanline's attempt to slay this woman, and that party's subsequent dispatch by her brothers. And this shooter you see is Hanline's .45 calibre Walker Colt which

18

you will discover is the gun that pumped six slugs into Jubal Creech's body. Hanline is also believed responsible for the wounding or death of one of two Creech henchmen who pursued him from the Running M Ranch on the night of the killing. The second man was wounded and is currently recovering at Dog City jail, but has given verbal testimony naming Hanline as his employer's murderer whom he pursued from the scene of the crime until overtaken by loss of blood.'

It was fascinating to witness the hanging judge seeming to crumple in upon himself, incapable of registering anything but brute shock and bitter disappointment as relief and exuberance exploded all about him. Then the star of the drama threw up her arms for silence, and smiling fiercely like the big sleek cat she was, cheerfully confessed she'd loved bad Jubal and would miss him sorely. She went on to reveal that she been content to let matters rest as they were after Hanline finally fell under her kinsmen's guns in Dog City, until made aware of what was happening here in Sweetwater.

She paused to turn the full candlepower of that dangerous smile upon the men up in the dock.

'Howdy there, my pretty chickadees. Just imagine, us four was all dancin' the cucaracha at the Fallen Angel together Monday night . . . but what a fish-fry of troubles we've seen since.'

The accused smiled hugely. The judge make a choking sound in his throat. Rebecca tossed her mane like a proud stud-mare before revealing a winsome sense of responsibility towards Cassidy, Pike and Waco.

'When the sheriff at Dog Creek told me you crazy people here had gone and charged these baby-faced wild boys with cancelling old Jube, I couldn't believe my ears.'

She shrugged, and there wasn't a male in the place not distracted by the way she did it. 'So naturally I had to convince my brothers that we all had to hustle down here with our evidence and save their cute little cabooses.' She winked. 'Guess you'll be grateful to Beckie Baby, huh my little darlin's? I mean, real grateful, huh?'

The hanging judge was last seen shuffling from the courtroom leaning heavily on his hangman's shoulder a short time later. Justice had been done here in this place on that memorable day, but the hate-blinded old man had played no part in it, was all too well aware of that fact as he was taken off in search of rye whiskey and oblivion.

Which prompted someone to suggest everyone take a drink. It may have been the sheriff.

Daybreak. Time to ride. The Kentuckians were heading south, so it was rumored.

'What's south, for Pete's sake?' quizzed the Mississippi gambler, his voice roughened by cigars. 'Just one muddy river after another. Redskins and sodbusters, nothing else. And if that ain't bad enough, if you keep pushin' south you'll hit Texas, for God's sake. They're thinkin' mebbe Texas'll suit them better than Colorado? They gotta be dreamin'!'

Sore heads nodded in agreement as last night's guests of honor, looking fresh and chirpy, clattered down from upstairs with warbags over their shoulders to say goodbye.

'Never too late to change your minds and stay, hunky-chunks.' It had been Rebecca's night also. She'd howled at the moon as long and loud as anybody, but had danced off the drink and looked robust enough to party on, dawn till dusk.

'Sorry,' Cassidy said simply. 'Got to be this way, folks.'

'We're looking to go ranching,' Waco felt obliged to explain with a lopsided grin. 'After yesterday you know. Settle down and keep out of trouble, would you believe?'

The sun broke free of the hills as three horsemen clattered out of Main to swing onto the South Trail over Morgan's Bridge.

Squinting in the hurting brightness, new friends and old were predicting certain failure and fiasco for their rapidly disappearing best pards, as they watched them recede into the distance. Only one man saw things differently as he pinned on his star and smiled around the first cigar of the new day.

The sheriff's voice was soft; 'Burn while you can, boys. Plenty time to toast your toes, grow a fat belly and answer "yes ma'am" later.'

Then they were gone and the sheriff sighed as he turned away to face a life which seemed suddenly so much smaller now and somehow gray.

2
The River Rider

Two mornings later saw the partners sitting down to a Brazos River breakfast at the Merion Steakhouse and calculating that they might just have enough in their Levis to meet the $1,500 asking price for Turtle Ranch, Comanche Hills, Buffalo County as advertised on the newspaper-clipping Cassidy drew from his shirt pocket half-way through their steaming pot of Campfire Coffee.

'We could likely get it for under,' Abe predicted. He read aloud: ' "Modest improvements, good water, needs work and fencing".' He glanced up. 'Doesn't sound like Rancho Grande, I'll admit,' he grinned. 'But what can you expect for $1,500?'

'Sour soil, fifty miles from town, freezin' in the winter and most likely rustler troubles all year round, is what. That'd be my guess from what I know of the Comanche Hills,' supplied a Merion old-timer when he overheard Cassidy repeat his rhetorical question in the supplies store some time later. He scratched a match into life on the scarred metal belly of the fat iron stove and set the tiny flame to a heavy curved pipe, eyeing them shrewdly over the bowl. 'Good enough for hard scrabble rancher folk mebbe, but – and don't take this personal – but you young roosters don't seem to fit that definition, wouldn't you agree?'

They scowled and hefted their purchases to wander outside into the morning sun.

'You reckon he's right?' Waco frowned as they stood outside the store where the new day was just beginning to pick up momentum in rip-roaring Merion.

Waco appeared pensive as he scratched his belly-button through a gap in his shirt; he was a supple-bodied man with square jaw and curly dark hair.

'You reckon he could be right?' he asked pensively. 'I mean, sure, we've worked on plenty ranches, know more about horses and cattle than most folks. But does that make us cattlemen? Mebbe we should hold out for something better, easier. . . ?'

'I guess Old Pops sounded like he knows what he's talking about, I'll allow,' Pike conceded, jerking his head at the doorway.

'You two beat all,' Cassidy snapped, strapping sacks to the saddle horn with the short-tailed chestnut trying to nip his backside. 'We dodge a hangrope, make a solemn agreement and ride a hundred miles to do a thing, then as soon as some pot-belly old porch-loafer throws a little cold water you want to turn belly-up . . .'

His voice trailed off as he realized the sagebrush sage had followed them out, trailed by a couple of seedy sidekicks.

'Sticks and stones, sonny,' he said sourly, sucking a great draught of thick tobacco smoke into his lungs. 'But I guess young boneheads like you'll always make a mock of good advice, and gotta make your own mistakes.' He paused to squint down at tight-lipped Abe. 'So, did I hear you say you ain't headin' through Hardrock but plan to cut across country for the hills direct, young shaver?'

Hands on hips, hat thrust back, Cassidy nodded firmly.

'Sale's on tomorrow, sixty miles if you go through Hardrock, or well and under forty miles by hitting due south,' he affirmed. 'We might just barely make it even taking the shorter route.'

The oldster glanced at his stooges to make sure they were paying attention. 'What about the rivers?' he demanded.

'What about them?' Waco challenged.

'It's been rainin' out yonder over the Ratenal Mountains for two days solid, is what,' the man said, stabbing his pipestem in a south-westerly direction where dark mountain ranges fanged the sky. 'Rivers flow west to east this part of the country, in case you don't know. That means the Canadian, the Zapolite and Silver should all be in rip-roaring full flood by the time you get down there, so you can forget about gettin' up into the Comanches for another two or three days.'

He grinned with smug self-satisfaction as he swaggered off with his retinue. 'But don't let a pot-bellied old porch-loafer spoil your fun, buckos. You know best. You're young, so you know everythin'. Good trailin' and ranchin', haw haw!'

'No!' Cassidy snapped as two questioning faces swung his way. 'Nobody else has said anything about floods. We can reach Mantrap Basin by first light tomorrow if we don't dally, and be at the Turtle by auction time at nine – which is just what we are going to do.'

So saying, he fitted foot to stirrup and swung up. Goober, eager for the trail, jumped out into the center of the street, wagging his tail. Waco and Pike traded glances, took another look at their partner's tight-jawed face, sighed and headed for their mounts. Sometimes, when easy-going Abe Cassidy adopted his familiar 'Raccoon River scowl', it was far easier to go along with him than dig in.

But spirits lifted as soon as they were out on the wide buffalo plains with the tough and runty mustangs travelling smooth as silk beneath them, running like they never wanted to stop.

A gentle wind in their faces seemed to bring new and unfamiliar scents of the south, hinting at places and peoples of the west they'd never yet seen. A turquoise-colored sky. A few fluffy clouds stood glaringly white against the awesome depth of color. Sure, there was a dark rain haze still clinging to the Ratenals. But on such a magic day it just wasn't possible to imagine floodwaters and washouts, much less fret about having to deal with them.

Sundown found them thirty-five miles due south. They sat their lathered horses on a high grassy bank between a pair of twin cottonwoods and stood drinking in their first sight of Silver River. It wasn't easy to miss. Well over a hundred yards wide at this point, the Silver was in full, tumultuous bank-to-bank flood, a mighty torrent of ochre-colored water that roared like Niagara as it went churning on its mission south-east to feed the parched Canadian.

It was impossible to make oneself heard above the tumult. But that was no problem. Right now, there didn't seem to be much anyone wanted to say, least of all Abe Cassidy.

'Looks even wider here,' remarked Waco as they reined in some ten minutes later a mile downstream.

'And deeper,' grunted Pike.

Both men looked at Cassidy, all three bathed in the golden afterglow of day flooding the western sky. They were halted on a knoll far enough back from the river to be able to make themselves heard, yet Abe still felt he had not much to say one way or another. He was thinking less of old Pot-Belly being right about the rivers than the all too obvious fact that if there was no way they could cross the Silver this in turn meant Turtle Ranch would go under the auctioneer's hammer without them.

He sighed as he cut a sideways glance at the others. Maybe it was best, he reflected. Maybe making such a major decision as they had done, hard on the heels of what they'd gone through in Colorado, wasn't all that smart after all. Could be they really weren't ready to settle and quit their rambling, although for a while there he'd been dead-set convinced they were.

Afterwards, they reasoned it must have been the dinning sound of the river that enabled the rider to come right up behind them without being heard. Even Goober seemed unaware of the new arrival, and the three horsemen started and whirled on hearing the easy south-western drawl right in back of them.

'Evenin', gents. Some sweet-lookin' sunset, huh?'

The man sat the saddle of a bottle-nosed mustang, not much different from their own mounts. He was young and tow-headed with an easy-going look about him despite the big walnut-butted Colt revolver sagging lop-eared from a cutaway holster on his hips. His grin was sunny and boyish.

'Never meant to startle you gents.' He snapped his fingers at Goober as he started towards him, and the big dog immediately squatted back on his haunches. 'Good dog,' he said amiably. He lifted fingers to hatbrim as he met their puzzled stares. 'Live hereabouts. Sighted you comin' along the river and got the notion you're lookin' for a way across.'

'Dead right,' said Pike. 'Got business up in the hills in the morning, but looks like it'll have to wait.'

'Well, I agree that might've well been the case if I hadn't lucked along, pardners.'

'Huh?' said Waco. 'You saying you know a way across, stranger? Looks blamed impossible to us.'

'Everything's impossible until you've done it,' came the laconic reply as the stranger pointed his horse downstream. 'Follow me. We need to make the fordin' afore darkdown.'

They followed readily enough. There was a huge bend in the river a short distance on, and to save time their guide led them across country a mile to pick it up again where the Silver began to narrow as it ran between rising cliffs. The Kentuckians looked dubious. Seemed to them if the river narrowed it must flow even deeper and faster. But they kept on after their man anyway and were glad they did. Another half-mile trailing the black-tailed mustang, and suddenly the cliffs widened and flattened some and the Silver looked somehow less challenging here to their trailwise eyes.

The young man reined in, indicated a big yellow tree on the far bank.

'For some reason the riverbed rises along here. The current's faster, sure, but it's no more than horse-belly deep. With rock underfoot a man can make it across here even at full flood providin' he keeps a tight rein and watches his footin' careful.' He turned with a cocked eyebrow. 'Game?'

They conferred. The river still looked pretty treacherous, yet there was something very reassuring about their youthful guide.

At last Luke Pike said, 'I'm for it.' He turned to the young man. 'We need to reach Mantrap Valley by mid-morning . . .'

'There's a game-trail cuts up left of that big old spur shaped like a fryin' pan,' he was told. The man nodded to Friendly and Waco. 'You'll make her easy, but you'd best get movin' now if you're goin'.' His easy smile showed. 'I can't make any guarantees about this here crossin' if you try her after dark.'

They looked at the sky. The light was fading fast. The Silver growled in its rocky bottoms. Nodding their thanks to the young man who was rolling a brown paper quirly one-handed, they pushed reluctant horses into the water and immediately felt the river's sullen strength.

It was no simple task crossing the Silver, yet at no stage did the riders feel endangered. Everything the man had said proved out; the water never rose higher than stirrup-length and strong horses were able to handle the current.

Surging up on the far bank, they were laughing and relieved as they swung their horses to face back the way they'd come, ready to give their Samaritan a big Kentucky yell of appreciation.

The north bank was deserted, the mile-wide sweep of rock and shale beyond showing no sign of life.

'I be dogged!' Waco said. 'Where in hell did he get to so fast?'

'Well, he's gone and we've got miles to go before we sleep, man,' Cassidy replied, slapping wet reins. 'Let's dust.'

Almost immediately they found the well-worn animal trace cut by critters coming down to drink. As they climbed, they glanced back from time to time in the deepening gloom but saw no sign of the man on the gray mustang. They didn't think much more about it then, where he'd come from, what he'd done for them and the way he just seemed to vanish from sight. But in time they would.

The barrel-bodied auctioneer from Hardrock was skilled enough at his trade to be almost able to convince canny old cowmen that a bone-dry longhorn cow was a lively heifer capable of producing an unending line of prime beef calves for their brand and lay the foundation for their fortune.

But even this fast-talking optimist found himself showing considerable restraint when it came to the task of applying the best possible sheen on Lot 15, namely Turtle Ranch with its advertised 'improvements, stock, water-supplies and fencing.'

'Solid as they come,' was his understated way of describing the headquarters to the small bunch of potential buyers who'd shown up at isolated Mantrap Valley to see Hodges' place go under the hammer. 'Sure, needs the handyman's touch here and there, and a little paint and fancy fixin's wouldn't go astray inside. But all in all a fine buy for the right buyer, no mistake about that.'

Trouble was, with a thin rain drizzling down and an uneasy wind blowing off the mesa which fed several small streams into the valley, the ranch's deficiencies were glaringly apparent, so much so that even the salesman's restrained spiel still seemed overstated.

The ranch house itself was fair to average in a rough-planked and jerry-built kind of way, but the outbuildings looked like a good blow would send them over. Hodges was no cattleman or handyman, and it showed. The 'herd', as the auctioneer described it, seemed to comprise a couple dozen scrawny beeves, dimly visible through the veil of rain as they stood staring in brute curiosity at all the unfamiliar activity.

The fences were busted and Hodges conceded guiltily that the cabin roof needed 'fixin' some.' Fifteen hundred US dollars appeared a somewhat inflated price when a man took a good look at Turtle Ranch, yet when he opened the bidding at this advertised price the auctioneer found he didn't need to try to whip up any further interest.

'Here!' called the big man taking shelter on the cabin gallery, and everyone turned to stare at Judson Drake, owner of sprawling Pawnee Ranch down on the plains and the biggest man in Buffalo County.

'Why, thank you kindly, Mr Drake,' the fat man beamed, water trickling down his neck beneath his leaking umbrella. 'Er, ah . . . any advance on fifteen hundred?'

There followed a hurried conference between the three strangers on the edge of the crowd. Then Clem Waco lifted his arm and called, 'Fifteen hundred and ten!'

'Fifteen ten?' The auctioneer appeared amused, then peeved. 'We don't have increments of ten dollars on a property of this value, mister. You want to make that a decent bid?'

'Who are these people?' Judson Drake demanded around a fuming cigar.

'Never seen them afore, Mr Drake,' said a flunkey. He turned his head. 'Ash, you know anything about these fellers?'

The cattle king's long-haired bodyguard, with an ankle-length-Mackinaw slung over his shoulders, arched an eyebrow in the trio's direction. He shook his head. 'Want them moved on, boss?'

'Damnit, no!' Drake snapped. He raised his riding-crop and called, 'Two thousand dollars, auctioneer! Take it or leave it!'

A buzz ran through the small crowd. What could be ailing Judson Drake? If this double section of unremarkable high country was worth two thousand then none of those present was any kind of judge.

But the auctioneer standing on the crate under a leaking black umbrella was certainly not about to question the cattle king's judgement.

'I'm bid two thousand!' he trumpeted. 'Any advance? Two thousand once, two thousand twice—'

'Jest hold your fire a minute, sonny! I wanna speak to these jokers.'

All eyes switched to owner Hodges as he stepped down off the end of the dripping porch to make his bow-legged way towards the Kentuckians. The rancher was a tough and solitary old sidewinder, set in his ways, and it was well known that he'd never had any time for silver-haired Judson Drake.

'Is he nuts or something?' the auctioneer fretted. 'He'll lose this bid if the old fool isn't careful.'

'Who the tarnation are you?' Hodges demanded, ranging up before Waco, Cassidy and Pike. 'Are you biddin' or just foolin'? Well?'

'Does this look like we're fooling?' Waco challenged, digging into a leather valise to produce fat wads of worn banknotes. 'Sure we're serious.'

'Or were,' Cassidy said glumly, hat tilted against the drizzle. 'Fifteen fifty's all we've got—'

'I'll take it.'

They stared at the rancher as the auctioneer jumped down off his crate and sloshed their way, red-faced and anxious.

'You'll take five hundred dollars less?' Abe couldn't conceal his incredulity, and it was his turn to look peeved. 'What's your game, mister? You trying to make us look fools?'

'That man yonder,' Hodges stated, jabbing a bony finger at the group on the gallery, 'is one of the main reasons I'm up and quittin' the hills. Drake's a grabber and a crook and couldn't lie straight in bed. Any more than I would if I was forced to sell to him. I've no notion why the owner of the biggest outfit in the county wants to own my poor piece of dirt, only know there can't be nothin' good behind it. It's yours for fifteen hundred dollars if you still want it. Advertised price.'

The auctioneer lumbered up. 'Mr Hodges, have you gone loco?' he almost shouted, thinking of his ten per cent commission.

Maybe he was. But crazy or otherwise, Hodges was still standing firm on his decision when the cattle king rolled up to the group under the canopy of the finest carriage in the county. A heated argument ensued in which the three wide-eyed newcomers took no part at all. Harsh words were exchanged between big rancher and ex-rancher, which left Judson Drake red-faced and angry as he finally swung upon the Kentuckians.

'All right, all goddamn right!' he growled. 'This old fool is selling to you cowboys, so I'll make my offer to you. Two thousand. You can make a five-hundred-dollar profit on your investment as quick as that.' He snapped his fingers. 'Take it or leave it, saddle-tramps.'

For some reason, they weren't even tempted. There was

something about threadbare Hodges that seemed genuine and straight, something about overbearing Judson Drake that gave the opposite impression. Maybe if he hadn't dubbed them tramps it might have gone differently. Or maybe not.

They didn't even have to confer on this one. Waco thrust the money at the auctioneer who seemed unsure whether to accept it or not. The lean bodyguard with long hair remained seated in the back of the carriage. Drake made as if to step down, but a sharp word from the cattleman halted him. Drake was plainly livid, yet his self-control was impressive as he flicked an icy eye at a smirking Hodges before focusing his attention upon the three grinning Kentuckians.

Cold and grating, he said, 'I don't know who you gentlemen are, don't wish to. But if you ever believed anything, believe that you've made the mistake of your stupid poor-boy lives here today. Jake!'

The bearded driver slapped the reins, the teamers hit the harness and the big rig was off, rocking from side to side over the rough Turtle Ranch turf, with the long-haired man staring back through the window and his four outriders travelling abreast in gleaming yellow slickers.

'Well, well!' the auctioneer exclaimed when he could find his breath. 'A tad edgy there for a piece, but a deal is a deal, as they say.' He put on his big phony smile for seller and buyers. 'Well, Mr Hodges, you made your point. As for you young roosters, I guess I can predict that you'll get to look back on today as the day you gained a good piece of property and made yourselves a real bad enemy.'

The way the Kentuckians laughed at this and pounded one another on the back as though equally pleased about the one achievement as the other, caused auctioneer and cattleman to stare glumly and enviously at one another through the falling rain. Was it possibly they'd ever been this young?

3
Cowboys

The crooked creek wound its way down out of humped and broken hills, cleaving through a narrow gash in the bleak façade of a granite cliff-face to gurgle its way along this deep draw before losing itself in late afternoon shadows. This was a bleak and lonesome section of the Comanche Hills, many miles from Mantrap Valley and 3,000 feet above the plains, haunted at night by wolves and coyotes and sometimes grazed during the days by wild goats and cattle.

Deep within the almost impenetrable brush choking the upper end of the gullywash there showed a faint flicker of movement. It was a hairy ear flicking away a horsefly. The rest of the russet-colored wild longhorn, all the sun-dappled, one thousand pounds of mischief-on-the-hoof of him, from scimitar horns to burr-knotted tail, remained frozen motionless and almost indistinguishable from its brushy surrounds.

But the cow-hunters were seeing sharper than ever on this, their third day spent scouring the high country for wild stuff. They'd seen something and were reacting accordingly.

Luke Pike occupied the high ground some 200 feet above the draw where a runty aspen afforded perfect cover for man, dog and rat-tailed dun. The lanky Kentuckian was grinning in the shadow of his sweat-stained Stetson, an unlit cigarette clamped between his teeth. There was nothing like the thrill of the hunt for this son of a Baptist preacher from Frog Hollow, West Kentucky. Didn't matter to him whether it was puma, grizzly, wolf or renegade longhorn bull, it was all the same to him. Exciting.

It was Pike who'd finally cut the sign of the bull and his harem up here, 1,000 feet above their valley, but having tracked their quarry down he was now waiting for Waco to signal the next move. They were taking it in daily turns to be 'straw boss' on this, their second week of saddle busting, body-bruising hunt for brush cattle to boost the Turtle's meager herd, and today Waco was in charge and loving it.

Pike looked for Waco but couldn't sight him. That was because he'd concealed his compact frame and short-tailed chestnut beneath a rocky overhang due west of the draw and slightly below it, from which point he'd had to stand in his stirrups to catch his glimpse of that one little ear flick.

Times like this Clem Waco could scarce suppress his exhilaration either. Sure, they were learning to work and behave like regular sober-sided ranch folk should, as time went by and the full weight of responsibility made itself felt. But at moments like this, out on the hunt and with the quarry close at hand, it was impossible not to want to just bust loose and go for it with all you had as they'd done so often in what were already shaping up in their minds as the good old days.

But he managed to hold back even though his mount was champing at the bit, sensing the rider's excitement. He had to wait until Abe showed himself. For this was a full three-man operation. They must first get the bull in order to get the cows. If that big rogue bested them again they'd be returning to headquarters empty-handed.

Where was that towheaded 'Coon Creeker anyway?

The answer to this was . . . surprisingly close by. Anticipating how Waco would go about this operation, Cassidy had spent several laborious minutes easing his cayuse quietly up through the sycamores flanking the northern rim of the draw, from which point he was now leaning forward in his saddle, peering through spring fronds to assess the exact position of their hidden quarry, and even more importantly, to survey the draw itself.

When the drama began the draw would be the stage. There was no place else for that bull to go.

He licked dry lips on catching a faint glint of light coming off twin horntips set six feet apart. The longhorn had escaped from Turtle Ranch a year earlier, defying all efforts to reclaim him. They needed this bunch-quitter badly, for there was nothing left in the kitty to splash around buying stock.

It took him a time to finally detect Waco's dim mounted outline in the shade of the overhang. He lifted a finger to hatbrim . . . which was all Clem Waco had been waiting for.

A light touch of spur saw the muddy-colored roan explode from beneath the shelf of rock, Waco's 'Yeehaaah!' slamming to and fro between the cliffs like a Kiowa battle cry.

A violent upheaval trembled the brush and next

moment the longhorn shot into the open at full throttle, heading along the creek like it was on tram tracks as it made for the timber cover beyond ... exactly as its tormentors expected.

They converged from three sides, riding hands and heels and yelling at the top of their lungs to confuse the critter further in the hope of causing it to do something foolish.

The bull had been hunted too often for that. Head down and tail rigidly upright, it stuck to its course, eating up distance in a storming charge which would surely have carried it clear of the draw and into the beckoning woods, but for Waco and his rope.

It was a dazzling throw which saw the lasso settle round the horns, then snap tight as Waco whipped the rope's end round the cantle and hauled his horse back on its heels. The rope snapped taut and the bull went up in the air like a Rocky Mountain trout hitting a lure.

As the longhorn hit ground, Waco brought his horse alongside ... and dived.

Closing in fast on either side, Cassidy and Pike couldn't believe it as their partner seized two deadly horns, swung his limber legs under the slobbering muzzle, hollered 'Yeeha!' again, then twisted with all his strength.

He'd roped the beast fair and square, but, Waco-like, had decided to bulldog it into submission. All one thousand pounds of him.

The tactic came as much of a surprise to the longhorn. It was caught off guard, which enabled Waco to achieve a full and vicious head twist before man and beast hit the ground in a crunching, turf-ripping slide that left a fifteen-foot scar along the draw bottom.

The longhorn's organ-toned bellow shook the treetops

as the beast struggled to rise. It didn't stand a chance. Once a strong man can get a beast downed with its neck crooked way back over, it is all through. Waco knew it, as did a laughing Cassidy and Pike as they sprang from their saddles with hopple-ropes in hand, while a triumphant Goober joyously barked right in the captive's face.

The rest was routine. Hoppled, head-hanging and smothered in dirt, the bull began its long downhill journey back towards Mantrap Valley and the fences. The beast trailed along in slobbering submission behind Waco, who was puffing on a cheroot and swaggering cockily, as he tended to do at such times. Cassidy and Pike brought up the rear, feeling real good.

They'd travelled about a mile before they heard a sound higher up in the trees. Pike jerked on the lead rope and the bull lurched to a halt. They waited. It wasn't long before the heifer poked her head into sight between twin pines. The longhorn gave tongue and the light-shanked little cow trotted down docilely to fall in alongside its lord and master.

By the time they raised the home acres at the end of their best day on Turtle Ranch, the home herd had been augmented by five: one bull, an old cow, two white-faced heifers and a dogie calf.

If this didn't call for some kind of celebration they didn't know what did.

The stars looked down. Cassidy, leaning on the top rail of the horse corral which was serving as a holding yard tonight, watched the dim shapes of the wild cattle moving quietly about inside and smiled again at their luck.

As he turned away he became aware of the weariness, the heaviness of his limbs, the new calluses on his palms and the big bruise he'd suffered in a tumble from his horse the previous day.

Ranching, as they'd always suspected, was proving to be a rugged business.

He headed for the lights. The partners had been on a fourteen-hour-a-day schedule since ever Hodges had signed over the deeds to them a fortnight earlier. You could see the improvements by day but by night the headquarters looked pretty much as it had done the first day, down at heel, isolated, a frail little outpost defying the elements and all the enemies natural to the big country.

Mantrap was as far back in the Comanche Hills as settlement could reach. Scattered spreads, trapper camps and a timber outfit or two dotted the lonesome trail north up to the plains and Hardrock. But south of their spread. beyond the jaws of Clawhammer Rocks, faintly outlined against the starry skies, Jubilee Pass led the abrupt way down out of the hills on to the trackless wastes of Indian Prairie.

The further one got from civilization the cheaper the dirt. That was how things worked 'most everyplace, he supposed.

But Turtle had potential, as all three agreed. Great potential. Most important, the big old mesa which formed the eastern boundary boasted several generous springs which flowed from cracks and caves in its lower walls to form a natural dam at its base. From the dam ran the stream which eventually joined up with Turtle Creek, watering the truck garden on the way and affording the stock additional places to drink.

Water was the key to successful ranching anywhere, and they wondered sometimes if the spread's liberal supply might be the reason Judson Drake had wanted to get hold of it so badly.

Cassidy smiled for the second time in minutes, wryly this time. He had not only gotten to live like a rancher, he mused, he was beginning to think like one. Could this be the same Abe Cassidy who'd spent the best part of two years chasing trouble, excitement, easy money and good times across the West until just a few weeks ago?

He sobered as he halted. He stared northward in the direction of Hardrock, Merion, the railroads and the boom towns, the Indian country and the wagon trains hauling the hopeful migrants West. 'Not the West, Cassidy,' he corrected. 'Our West. Get it right.' For years they'd dreamed it, were now living it. It was even greater than they'd imagined.

He shucked his jacket and went in.

The coal-oil lamp had been lit. Cassidy hung his hat on one of the wooden pegs driven into the slab wall and glanced toward the galley. The coffee-pot was on the stove but there was no other sign of culinary activity. His belly growled. It had been a long day. The longest.

The room was long with a roomy fireplace on one side, and a beamed, low ceiling that cleared Luke Pike's head by no more than a few inches. Pike was drinking coffee and staring out the window. Sprawled against the wall on the battered old couch, Waco was struggling with his harmonica, trying unsuccessfully to coax it to deliver 'Red River Valley'.

'What happened to chow?' Cassidy wanted to know.

'Coffee's on,' grunted Pike.

'What else?'

'Last night's beef and beans. We ain't heated it up yet.'

'Why not?'

41

Waco lowered his harmonica. 'What are you, man, a housewife or something? We never heated it on account we've had beef and beans three nights in a row, is why.'

'I'm up to here with beef and beans,' Pike complained, hunkering down to massage his dog's battle-scarred ears. 'What a man really wants is—'

'Town,' Cassidy cut in.

'Huh?' both said together. Their plan had been to work four weeks straight to get the place in some sort of shape, then head down to Hardrock for a blowout. It was Cassidy who'd originally outlined this plan and insisted on its acceptance. So what did he mean by 'town' – after barely two weeks?

He explained. 'We're overdoing it, is what. Look at us. We've just had three big days camping out chasing mossy-horns all over these crummy hills, eating hardtack and washing it down with cheapjack joe. Today we get lucky, come back with a lot more than even we hoped for – and look at us. Bad-smelling, bad-tempered and facing another hard-slog day tomorrow. Look, we're ranchers, for Pete's sake, not Mississippi chain-gangers. So, okay, we don't want to raise hell anymore. Fine. But does that mean we want to get to be old and crabby ahead of our time like that big old mossyhorn we snared today? Well, does it?'

That settled it. Tomorrow was pronounced a holiday. They'd be up before first light and in town by the time the saloons opened. There was a rush for the kitchen and first use of the razor. Hardrock – and just the faintest echo of the siren song of the good old days – was calling loud and clear.

The bullet smacked into the rusted tin roof of the stables just as Cassidy was leading his ugly chestnut outside by the first gray light of morning.

He didn't know it was a bullet until the vicious spang of a high-powered rifle carried down from the mesa a split second later.

He whirled as Pike and Waco came legging it across the yard. 'I saw a puff of smoke up by that fissure!' Waco bawled, vaulting astride his mustang. 'Let's get the varmint, goddamnit!'

In moments they were up and riding, angry-faced and with six-guns in hand but crunched low in their saddles in expectation of more bullets.

There weren't any. They made the steep, twenty-minute climb without incident to reach the fissure, where a quick search located a single spent .32 cartridge and the tracks of two horses in a small patch of earth amongst the rocks. Of course they were thinking it had to be the Pawnee. They had no other enemies in the county, hadn't really had the time or opportunity to make any.

They spent an hour scouring the mesa surrounds without finding anything further, and it was three grim-faced men who made the descent to the spread, where they loped across the pasture to swing down at the stables with the intention of inspecting the roof.

They didn't get that far.

It was Goober who alerted them with a strange kind of whine and Pike pivoted sharply to see the man seated on the top step of the cabin rolling a cigarette one-handed.

'I be dogged!' he gasped, Colt half out of the leather. 'Who the. . . ?' His voice cut off. He stared. 'Hey, ain't that the feller who. . . ?'

'Him all right,' cut in a tight-lipped Waco. 'The joker from the river. What's he doing here?'

They headed across to find out. The young man greeted them with a sunny smile around a freshly lit

43

durham, leaned back and scratched his flat belly luxuriously like an old man readying for a long day of doing very little.

'How do, pardners,' he greeted. 'Who's been shootin' you up?'

They halted at the bottom step, staring. Baby-faced and relaxed looking as a tabby cat on blanket, the man none the less had a glint in his eye that hinted he was serious today, maybe even real serious.

'You saw what happened?' Cassidy frowned. 'Where were you . . . er, what'd you say your name was?'

'What's in a name I always say.' The man rippled to his feet and suddenly had a six-gun in either hand, yet none had seen him draw. As they jumped back in alarm he transferred the cigarette from one corner of his mouth to the other with the tip of the tongue then descended to the yard, Colts angled at the ground. 'Pardners, just how good do you handle those shooters of yours? I need to know on account of from what we just saw you're goin' to need to be able to defend yourselves, wouldn't you allow?'

Mostly they liked things that happened fast; but this whole thing seemed to be going way too fast.

All three began talking at once but the young man was shaking his head. 'No, you don't get it. Don't tell me, show me.' He pointed. 'That big old gray stump Hodges should've snigged out, but didn't. Two shots apiece and I'll tally the score. You first, Abe.'

He was ordering them about yet somehow it didn't seem to offend. They'd noticed the night at the river that he seemed to have the natural authority of a far older man, yet there wasn't a line in his face.

When he drew a line in the dirt with the toe of his boot, Abe obediently stepped up to it, took aim and fired off two shots. Pike and Waco followed suit. They never did learn their tally, but the young man made it plain they could do with some improvement.

'Thing is,' he drawled, replacing his guns in their holsters, 'do you want help to lift your game, or am I hornin' in where I ain't welcome?'

Their responses were swallowed by thunderous gun blasts as he cleared his Colts again and almost knocked the scrawny stump out of the ground with a fusillade of bullets.

They stared at one another through the smoke. Guns had never played a major part in their lives, not handguns at least. But in light of what had happened here, perhaps that had been an oversight.

What followed was hour after hour of genial yet relentless tuition as the young man took them through marksmanship, the clear and draw and something he called the 'headwork' of gunmanship, which he kept insisting was the most important element of all.

'Doesn't matter how fast or slow you are, you make sure of just one thing; hit what you're shootin' at. Just about every man-jack who fancies himself shoots too fast. And most who shoot too fast miss. I've had slugs sprayin' all round me but come away with the money just because I made sure, dead sure you might say, that what I aimed at I hit. That's headwork and now we are goin' to work on that. I mean really work.'

He didn't lie. The hours that followed were intensely concentrated as, with infinite patience, their tutor took them through their paces time and time again until they felt they were getting worse by the minute. Yet he appeared quite satisfied with the results by the time he whistled up his mustang and reloaded his guns before swinging up.

He touched hatbrim. '*Vaya con Dios, amigos.* Keep sharp, keep practicin', and I'll see you when the grapes get ripe.'

They felt like schoolkids seeing off their teacher as he loped away, and there was a whole mess of things they wanted to ask and know about. Such as why he bothered going out of his way to help them out, where he'd learned to shoot that way, and certainly who he was even if he did consider names unimportant.

It had been a strange yet somehow exhilarating day and they sat talking on the stoop and sipping coffee until dusk when somebody remembered their decision to go to town.

There was a rush for the two razors again. Pike lost out so elected to saddle the horses once more. As he led them across the yard in the gloom he crossed the spot where the young man had ridden out. He stood staring thoughtfully at the tracks and massaging his jaw. This was twice now the youthful horseman had shown up out of nowhere to come to their assistance. He wondered who he might be. Some kind of Buffalo County Good Samaritan, perhaps? Mostly this lanky Kentuckian didn't trust nameless strangers until he found out what made them tick over. Yet with the rider of the brushtail, it seemed a man was ready to put his confidence in him right from the jump. Curious that.

But he didn't bring up the subject of the mysterious kid when he went inside. Didn't feel like talking serious on such a fine night with town beckoning and a new-found confidence in their gun capability which seemed to counterbalance their anger at being fired upon earlier.

They made record time to Hardrock. It was the only way they knew.

4
Young and Fast

There was nothing remarkable about Hardrock now that
its wild days seemed to be behind it. Three stores, a livery,
five saloons and a fifth that was called a hotel because they
rented rooms, a jailhouse and a hundred houses encom-
passing several square blocks. Surrounded by reaching
plains, the town regarded itself now as hard-working,
conservative, in sharp contrast with its turbulent origins,
although life could still be pretty rough and basic along
the street they called The Line. It was almost noon when
the marshal quit the law office and made his way along the
weather-buckled sidewalk for the Three Deuces Saloon.

'He's right on time,' murmured the pot-bellied store-
keeper, surveying the street from his shadowed doorway,
watching the lean figure go by. 'Same time every day. *These*
days, that is. . . .'

People noticed things this week that would have
seemed unremarkable just a short time ago. Things like
balcony loafers constantly watching the plains through
field-glasses and telescopes, or their formerly teetotal

marshal falling into the habit of predictable and regular visits, to the Deuces, for instance.

Until recently life in Hardrock had seemed suppressed maybe, yet reassuringly straightforward and predictable, particularly when viewed in contrast to just a couple of years back when Jimmy Kaine had 'reigned' as the youthful rebel king of the county, or before that when the Blind Fool Creek boys had locked in bloody battle with Judson Drake and Pawnee Ranch and lost.

Of course there was still the occasional Saturday night saloon ruckus to liven things up, and every now and again the county's favorite wanted son, wild Jimmy Kaine, could be relied upon to make the headlines just to remind everyone that there was still some fire in the communal blood. Nonetheless a sizable congregation showed up at the little white church on Maple each Sunday, regular as clockwork, and a woman could still walk down Maple safely after dark. In office over a year now, most everyone agreed the marshal had done a solid job during his term behind the badge.

Tell Dalton was a different man from his predecessor who'd had to deal with the major upheavals that had characterized Buffalo County's past. He'd missed entirely the murderous resolution of the Pawnee Ranch–Blind Fool Creek feud, had come in at the tail end of a colorful period when a twenty-one year old kid named Kaine had somehow gotten to champion the county's Have-Nots in their long struggle against the Haves. Kaine's eventual conviction on a suspect charge, resulting in his retreat into the hills, had seen the rich and powerful finally assume full command of the region, leaving little real responsibility for the new badgeman.

It was five years now since Dalton's predecessor had

freighted Kelso and his henchmen off to Territory Prison
– exactly five years, as the sheriff was only too well aware.

Lying on his office desk at that moment today was a
terse wire from the Warden of Territory, which read;

PRISONERS KELSO AND BLIND FOOL CREEK BOYS RELEASED
TODAY, SUGGEST FULL ALERT.

The lawman grimaced as he stood waiting on the
corner for a wagon to pass. The warning was scarcely
necessary, he mused. When Kelso stood in the dock the
day the survivors of the Blind Fool Creek bunch were each
sentenced to five years' hard, he'd sworn he'd been
framed, railroaded and gypped out of his land by Judson
Drake and had vowed vengeance with such ferocity that
nobody seriously doubted his sincerity.

Dalton was marshalling a tough frontier town on the
Panhandle at that time. But the detailed report on the
entire Blind Fool Creek–Pawnee Ranch affair was on file
at the jailhouse, and he'd studied it often enough over the
past few weeks to commit it to memory.

Small wonder this customarily abstemious badgeman
felt the need for a stiff shot around noon every day, with
boosters at regular intervals thereafter.

There were few in town who didn't anticipate serious
trouble when Kelso's bunch returned. It was no secret that
Judson Drake had bolstered his gun force out at the
ranch, and most who'd known Kelso agreed that this
would seem a smart thing to do. As Dalton understood the
situation, Kelso had been something of a troublemaker
and rebel whom prison had apparently forged into a truly
dangerous man obsessed by hatred.

Exactly what Tell Dalton didn't need just at a time when

there seemed to be so much going on in Hardrock that he didn't understand. Real estate was changing hands at a fire-sale rate and there were constant rumors that Judson Drake was engaged in some major secret project which might or might not be good for the region. The fact that Dalton had come to actually fear the Pawnee boss during his tenure didn't seem to augur well for his immediate future when it appeared certain Drake and Kelso might come together like a couple of freight trains.

He was thinking out loud when he muttered, 'When elephants fight the grass suffers.'

'Howdy, Marshal,' a deep voice interrupted his introspection as he crossed the street. 'Any news from up north?'

The blacksmith was runty but husky as his trade required. He looked nervous today, edgy. And the marshal thought: if the tough ones are getting jittery already, how are the rest faring?

'No news is good news, Mr Jones,' he said tersely and continued on for the Deuces, aware of the watching eyes, of the unnatural quiet, the feeling that something was about to happen.

'The hell with it!' he muttered, and thrust his way through the swinging doors into a welcoming, familiar world of tobacco smoke, strong liquor and painted women. Where the edge of reality was always a little blurred and where any man, even one wearing a five-pointed star, could find refuge from reality, a commodity Hardrock seemed overburdened by this mid-spring noon.

The glass was barely in the lawman's hand and the Professor had just swung back to his straight-backed piano on his swivel stool, flexing long bony fingers, when they heard it. The faint sound first mistaken for some fool rattling on a kettledrum someplace all too quickly evolved into the reality of hoofbeats hammering rhythmically on a hardpacked trail.

His whiskey half-way to his lips, Tell Dalton went very still, aware that every eye was now focused upon him. Every wide, fearful stare asking silently: Was it them?

There followed a sudden rush to batwings and windows as the plank bridge on the south trail trembled and gave off clattering echoes that sounded loud as gunshots as three hellions came storming across on lathered mustangs, whacking horsehide with their hats and howling like scalp-lifting Comanches.

Anxious citizens lining porches and walks were instantly relieved when they saw the youthful strangers in no way resembled jail-hardened hellions, or fearsome Injuns for that matter. Even so it took some moments to recover from their fright, in which time the riders vanished behind the bank, erupted again into Maple in a wide, swerving turn then came hammering towards the central block, almost skittling a big fat man in a blue railroad boilersuit doing the locomotive shuffle diagonally across the street.

The pedestrian squawked and stumbled in fright. Without missing a beat, Luke Pike changed direction fractionally to get a scooping hand under the railroader's armpit, straightened him up and left him teetering but safely upright and blinking after them while he lashed his cayuse after his friends through a pall of hoof-lifted dust.

It was impossible for them to ride without racing. This time Waco roared past the Three Deuces' hitch rail a good long nose ahead of Cassidy with Pike two horse-lengths behind.

As they turned to come trotting back, Hardrock had its first good look at the trio whom the realtor identified as the new owners of Turtle Ranch. Had it sighted the newcomers two days back, the town of Hardrock would have seen three unshaven, dust-coated horsemen drooping in their saddles from exhaustion as they herded a boogered bunch of scrub cattle down out of the hills to their spread. What they saw today were three exuberant youngsters busting with high spirits and cutting up like overgrown kids playing hooky as they sprang up onto the saloon porch to greet a stern-faced lawman like he was their best friend.

'Afternoon, Marshal sir. Sorry if we raised a little dust.'

'Right sorry, sir. Say, could you tell us something. Have we country boys come to the right place to buy us a mess of watered whiskey and be took down by shifty cardsharps and cheap wimmin?'

'Easy, easy,' Cassidy warned. He snapped a smart salute at a bemused Dalton. 'We're spooking our mint-new home town, can't you see, boys. Marshal, we're Cassidy, Pike and Waco from the—'

'I know – Turtle spread.' Dalton stared from face to face. 'You're the fellows who outbid Prairie Ranch for Hodges' place? You. . . ?'

But he'd lost them already. There were girls in the open doorway by this; no mistaking their gender, the skimpy way they were dressed. There were more directly across the street lined up prettily along the upstairs balcony of the faded pink building known simply as Lil's. To young men who seemed to have done nothing else over the past month but survive the most desperate kind of trouble, barely escaped being hanged, reached some momentous decisions, acted upon them and then worked like navvies day and night for the past two weeks – even been shot at – every single female looked like a living angel.

'Alleluia!' summarized the youngest and prettiest of Lil's Ladies as the swinging yellow doors of the Three Deuces closed upon the newcomers' eager backs. 'New blood at last.'

Slouched anonymous and unobserved against the door-frame of the Main Street Flophouse, a surly newcomer named Brown saw everything and said nothing.

'You comin' to the hoedown tonight, handsome?'

She was barely eighteen with bee-stung lips and a dancer's legs. Cassidy had never met a hoochie-coochie dancer he didn't like.

'Could be, darlin',' he grinned, leaning lazily against the bar. 'Where is it?'

'The lady said "handsome", pilgrim,' interrupted Pike. He tipped his hat to the girl, grinning down at her five-two from his six-three. 'Handsome at your service, miss. And you might as well know hoedown dancin' is my speciality.'

'His speciality is boring people to death,' cut in Waco, sliding an arm through the girl's and whisking her away. 'I heard them calling you Trixie. I knew a Trixie in Tennessee once. Her ma was a trick rider in the circus and her daddy was a snake hypnotizer. Any relation. . . ?'

His words were lost in the hum of conversation and clink of glassware filling the late afternoon bar-room. The new ranchers were a long way from liquored but were certainly relaxed, with the spread, chores, blisters, sunburn and gunshots comfortably fading and backgrounded as they continued to do what they had once done so well, and often. Namely have a damn fine time while getting to know their newly adopted town, which largely meant getting to know the Chief.

Chief Long Bear owned the Deuces and was the only

Indian saloonkeeper in five hundred miles. Tall and stately, sardonic and sharp as a straight-edge razor, the Chief presided over his smoky domain from behind a polished teak bar with the aplomb and acute observation of a mystic, yet he was a practical man who knew how many beans made five and how to make the giant leap from reservation Indian to success in the white man's world.

'You boys claim you're ranchers?' he challenged without any preamble as Cassidy and Pike resumed their high stools. 'I don't think so.'

'What?' Pike frowned, like he thought he'd missed something.

Chief Long Bear was as tall as Pike in a hand-woven Choctaw shirt and leathern pants. Shoulder-length hair was held back by a beaded headband. Big sorrel hands unhurriedly drew a beer and slid it down along the mahogany where it was fielded by a drunk with faultless reflexes.

'Runners would be my best guess,' he replied.

'Huh?' said Cassidy.

'So you've brought a ranch,' the Indian stated calmly. 'But from what you've already revealed to me of your life before coming here, I suspect you are still runners. You admit you have tried the towns, the riverboats, the buffalo camps and the mines. You've ridden shotgun for Butterfield, cold-camped in the Rockies and sold whiskey to reservation Indians. You say you quit Merion when it linked up with the Rimrock Line, then you headed south fast when the railroad began blowing woodsmoke all over you. Now you buy a no-account spread in the backblocks of creation and call yourselves settled-down cowmen. My prediction is this. The day the mailrider gets to go as far as your ranch regular you'll think it's getting too civilized

54

and you'll all up stakes and go looking to raise turkeys down on the Llano Estacado.' He shrugged. 'Runners.'

'Don't mind the Chief,' put in the girl with the broken-hearted smile. 'He talks funny sometimes. Don't you, Chief?'

'No,' Pike said soberly, 'he's driving at something. You're saying you don't reckon we've got what it takes, mister?'

'You miss my point. Most folks do. Listen carefully. If I stand here long enough everyone in the West will pass through those batwings eventually. I learn something from them all. I study men and read what is in them. You, brothers, are but boys, but you're Old West in here.' He tapped his chest. 'You don't like towns and don't cotton to railroads or cotton gins. Progress ... that's what you're running from. I see it all the time, just standing here. Men on the run and not even aware what they are running from. Most run from women or debt or disaster. But you fellows are rarer, different from most.'

'You will have to spell it out,' Cassidy insisted.

The Choctaw obliged.

'I have seen them even younger than you boys. Men yearning for a past and a life that's fast slipping away ... the Old West. There was one kid in particular like that, a fabulous boy ... but that doesn't signify now. What signifies is that most men don't know what they are fleeing from.' A big grin split the bronzed face. 'At least I've explained to you youngsters what fuels your boilers now, and I won't even charge you for the service.'

The two stared at him for a long moment of silence. Then Pike shoved his dog out of the road with his boot and got to his feet.

'Let's shift camp. If this reservation rotgut won't addle a man's brain his bulldust sure will.'

'On our way,' grunted Cassidy. He was eager for lots of things here but profundities weren't amongst them.

'You'll be back, gents!' the Chief called after them. He sounded sure.

The lamplighter was half-way through his rounds as they hit the street, the warm glow of the Rager lamps taking the harsher edges off this solid, hardbitten town of the plains. The partners walked, thumbs hooked in gunbelts and cigarettes jutting from their mouths, still slipping unconsciously back into cowboy style; it might well be a time before they learned to look, walk or even think like genuine cattlemen.

'Old West!' Pike muttered. Then he propped at a lighted store window to admire a fine leather jacket from Luber and Sons, Kansas City. 'How long before we can afford to flash up like that do you reckon, Abe?'

'Maybe not long,' Cassidy grunted as they moved on, absorbing the atmosphere and revelling in the sight of everyday folks and lamplit stores. A brief recollection of their close call in Colorado clouded his face, but was quickly gone. 'I get a rich feeling every time I think of those wild beeves we ran in. There's more up higher, you know, pard, I could smell them. Say, maybe that's what interested Mr Big!'

'Who?'

'Mr Big. Drake. Don't it puzzle you why he was busting to buy the Turtle when he owns more prime acres than we've seen hot suppers?'

'Speaking of which . . .' Pike grinned, and side by side they swung in beneath a stylishly lettered sign identifying a noisy frame-and-adobe building as Charlie's Greasy Spoon.

The eatery was crowded with punchers in denim and

leather, in for the night at the end of another week on the range. Two fat men in vast white aprons were hustling to and from the kitchen toting steaming platters of beef and beans and huge pan-fried steaks. They took chairs at a long table occupied by a bunch of grimed and bristled Texans heading back for the Pecos after delivering another herd to the Merion railhead, lean, weather-beaten fellows who seemed to like the cut of their jib and soon got to telling them of what the long trail had been like, as the waiters brought Pike and Waco sourdough flapjacks enlivened by huevos rancheros sauce.

'Pure hell,' declared a waddy no older than themselves, yet aged and drawn by four months living in a saddle. 'The boss man gets the big bucks, and what do we get? Twenty-one weeks fighting dust, hail and lightning. Times the cattle would stampede a dozen times in the one night. We fought jayhawkers, Kiowas . . . left Comanches dead in their own tall grass . . .'

The man's voice faded. He stared at nothing, seeing it all again in his mind; cruel, feathered images lined up against the cerulean blue of a Texas sky, smelt once more the blood and fear.

The Kentuckians traded glances. They were back to doing what they liked best, soaking up the excitement, color and violence of the West, the real 'Old West' as Chief Long Bear called it.

They were lingering over coffee after the Texans left, debating the wisdom of attending the hoedown at Jackson's Dining Rooms, when they became aware of a lessening in the buzz around them. They looked up. Two diners from the back of the room now stood by their table. One had cowhand stamped all over him, the other was lean, straight as a bayonet and familiar. Ash Pride had been with Judson Drake at the Turtle Ranch auction. Bodyguard and right-hand man, so they believed.

'Looks like they serve jest about anybody in this rathole these days, Ash.' The cowboy had a lisp. He was nervous, they could tell, but trying to act tough.

'Sure does.' Pride's ornate double gunrig was on Pike's eye level as he fingered his hat back from his forehead. 'You know, we figured you shavetails would be long gone from Turtle by this. Truth to tell, I'm kind of disappointed that ain't so.'

Pike and Cassidy traded looks. They weren't looking for trouble but sometimes weren't all that adroit at avoiding it either.

Cassidy managed a tight smile as he tilted his chair back against the wall and looked up at them, aware of the expectant quiet all about them.

'Right sorry about that,' he drawled. He was thinking of all the brawls he'd been in from Raccoon Creek to Buffalo County, many of which might have been better avoided, and yet the memory of sweet violence was strong. He motioned to the bottle on the table. 'Nothing like a shot for disappointment as old Granny Green used always to say back home. Eh, Luke?'

Pike was studying the Pawnee pair. The quietest of the trio mostly, he was not a good man to provoke.

'Sure,' he forced himself to say. 'Set and have a drink. We've got no hassle with you fellas.'

That wasn't how Ash Pride saw things. Leaning the knuckles of both hands on the table edge, he said deliberately, 'You're way out of your depth here, hicks. Mr Drake needs that piece of dirt you're camping on up there . . .'

'Why so?' Cassidy broke in sharply, getting to his feet. 'It's nothing much, as everybody knows, yet they say it takes two hours to ride across the Pawnee. What's your boss want with—'

'You don't have this straight, boy,' Pride said coldly, straightening from the table to let his arms hang loosely at his sides. 'You're not asking questions, I'm talking. And what I'm saying, real straight and plain, is that we want you off Turtle and Mr Drake is getting impatient about it. So when do we meet up to discuss a price? Mr Drake will be generous.'

'Blow it out your ears, jackass,' Pike rapped.

Cassidy was expecting something like this and so was ready. He was no gunner but yesterday's tuition by the young man from the river out at the spread had done wonders for his self-confidence. His right hand blurred and Charlie's Greasy Spoon froze tight as lamplight winked on the .45 in his fist. A fat waiter dropped a tray with a mighty clatter which emphasized the sudden hush. Cassidy's smile was sunny as a bluebonnet morning, but nobody was taken in by it.

'Your manners are lousy and your judgement is worse, hired help,' he declared. The gun muzzle waved at the door. 'We're peaceable folk but we don't let red-nosed hicks push us around. On your way. And better run tell your boss the Turtle isn't for sale. Hey, you still here?'

It seemed for a hanging moment that Pride might do something reckless. Then the cowboy silently touched his arm, the contact seeming to draw the venom out of the man, though he looked anything but relaxed as he tugged his hat down low and turned to leave.

'You'll regret this, hicks,' he hissed. 'Mr Drake is going to be real sore.'

'Give him our best,' Cassidy replied, contemptuously holstering and reaching for his hat before the pair were out the door. He flipped his hat and caught it. 'Good chow, Charlie!' he called to the ashen fat man staring out from his kitchen. Then, 'Don't look so jittery, folks. It's all over and we're leaving. Matter of fact we're heading for the hoedown if anyone cares to join us.' He winked at a pretty girl seated with a scowling teamster. 'Especially you, brighteyes.'

Normal sounds didn't return to the eatery until the hinged door had flapped to stillness behind them. Then everyone wanted to talk at once to ease the tension. They knew Ash Pride well in Hardrock, and the summary voiced by the red-nosed town mayor accurately reflected their general reaction to the incident just past.

'Guess them boys is likable enough,' he opined. 'And I don't reckon they mean no real harm even if that Cassidy kid does seem a tad too slick with an iron for my likin'. But they made a big mistake tonight. No man can buck Judson Drake and expect to sleep easy.'

None disagreed. Drake had come to the county just six years earlier, unknown and unheralded. Now he was the biggest man in the region, and independent as they might like to see themselves, the citizens of Hardrock knew he now virtually bossed their town almost as completely as he did Pawnee Ranch.

To a man, they felt sorry for the youthful newcomers to Mantrap Valley and wouldn't be in their boots for big dollars. Yet at that very moment, those boots and their owners were tapping and kicking flashily across the freshly waxed floorboards at Jackson's Dining Rooms to the rousing beat of 'Turkey In The Straw', seemingly without a care in the world.

5

Good Times and Fast Guns

Her name was Amanda and she didn't work at all, much less at saloons like the Deuces, or, perish the thought, across at Lil's. Indeed, her father was the preacher and her mother ran the library, which meant her credentials were impeccable. But the only credentials Cassidy was impressed by as they glided round cheek to cheek and heart to heart, was that she was gorgeous and seemed to have taken a real shine to him.

'I really should be going home,' she breathed warmly into his ear. 'What on earth time is it?'

He had no idea other than it was late. You could tell it was late by the thinning crowd and the condition of most of the dancers – nicely lubricated and feeling little pain.

Just like Abe Cassidy and friends.

They'd meant to head back early, of course. But a combination of Amanda, easy-going Western hospitality, a surprisingly good guitar band and dance floor plus Chief Long Bear dispensing liberally from a bar set up alongside the bandstand, found the Turtle Creek crew looking like they might get to dance down the moon and to hell with tomorrow's busy schedule.

But as the couple's dreamy way took them towards the bar, Cassidy felt the faintest prickle of conscience and was considering summoning his partners to hold a serious confab, when the Chief's big rich voice reached him;

'Come on, Jimmy-boy, if you want one last drink before we close up shop!'

'What's this "Jimmy-boy" stuff?' Cassidy asked his girl as they moved to take up the offer.

She shrugged pretty shoulders. 'Because you remind everyone of him, I guess.'

'Of who?'

'Why, Jimmy Kaine, of course. And I suppose you do at that. He was kind of cute too.'

Cute? Did he want to be cute? But he was frowning as he tried to place the name 'Jimmy Kaine', snapping his fingers impatiently until memory kicked in. Of course. They'd heard about him often in the past. Jimmy 'The Boy' Kaine was some kind of Western luminary here in the region where Texas, New Mexico and Oklahoma came together.

Then he recollected something else as the Chief handed him his glass. 'Hey, just a minute,' he protested. 'Before you get to handing out nicknames . . . this Kaine's an outlaw, isn't he?'

His question went unanswered as Amanda slipped her arm round his waist and hijacked him back on to the dance floor. 'Well, isn't he?' Cassidy insisted. 'A no-good, I mean.'

'Jimmy is just Jimmy,' she purred. 'Nearly as cute as you.'

'Everyone seems to know about him but us. Is this geezer dead or alive, or maybe just made up?'

She turned serious now. 'No, Jimmy lived . . . I knew him a long time ago . . .'

'So he's still alive?'

'Let us put it this way, handsome Abe. If he was alive he wouldn't just be standing back letting you monopolize me.'

'So, he's dead?'

'He could be. Who knows? Is it important?'

'Not to me it ain't.' Cassidy grinned, halting by the bandstand to slug down his whiskey. 'Anyway, from what I hear he must've been some kind of hardcase—'

'He's lots of things, *amigo*,' drawled a buck-toothed youth leaning against the bar. 'But mostly I guess what Jimmy Kaine is, is a friend. Yessir, any man what stood up against the big outfits like the banks, landlords, the law or the outlaws, you could bet Jimmy would be there to stand by him. Easy goin' man he is . . . but fight? Like a thresher he is. And nobody handles a hoss or a Colt like him, like the time he gunned down three *bandidos* tryin' to kidnap a gal up in the hills and—'

'Wait a minute, wait a dad-blamed minute,' interrupted a puzzled Cassidy. 'That gal there hints this geezer's dead, but you talk like he's alive. Which is it?'

'Amanda wants to think of him as dead and gone on account she don't get to see him no more 'cos he's on the dodge,' whispered a bystander. 'Makes it easier for her, I guess.' The drinker's eyes twinkled. 'But the Boy's hale and hearty, make no mistake. Take more'n the Grim Reaper to get the best of Jimmy Kaine, yessiree.'

Cassidy massaged his chin. There it was again. The same reaction he'd noticed before whenever that name came up, like it only took the words 'Jimmy Kaine' to capture everyone's attention and set their eyes shining. Didn't seem normal to him. Engrossing maybe, but weird.

'So alive, in truth,' added the drinker, 'that he done rode right on to Pawnee just ten days back and pinched back Joe Willis's appaloosa what some of them Drake waddies had stole offen him, claimin' it belonged to Pawnee.'

'Sounds like a hardcase to me,' Pike said in a bored voice.

'Wrong!' shouted a young waddy who'd been drinking with them, now leaping atop the bar. 'He is a dancin' fool, is what he is!' So saying, he launched himself into a staccato heel-smoking dance deftly avoiding bottles and customers with equal ease as the band provided a machine-gun backing for his furious routine.

'What the hell is this?' Pike had to shout to make himself heard.

'He's doin' the Jimmy Kaine!' laughed another of their party, and in mere moments everyone was performing the violently energetic dance-routine which went on and on until finally the band gave up and the dancers collapsed from simple exhaustion.

'I don't get it,' growled Pike. 'Are what you really sayin' is this Kaine is a dancer?'

'You want to know who Jimmy is?' slurred the guitar-playing singer, now reduced to sitting on the edge of the bandstand looking plenty the worse for wear. He strummed a chord. '*Really* wanna know?'

'He just loves to sing this song he wrote the night a crooked judge found Jimmy guilty of somethin' he never done and the Boy busted jail like it was made of wet paper,' chuckled a customer at Cassidy's elbow. Then he shouted, ' You bet we do, buddy!' Which started the whole room chorusing, 'Jimmy the Boy! Jimmy the Boy!'

The man with the guitar needed no second bidding; he had a good baritone voice even when seriously affected by rye whiskey. He sang;

Have you all heard the story of young Jimmy Kaine?
And the days when he ruled over mountain and
    plain
He wasn't a king but every man was his friend
'Cept the law and the rich man who brought his bad
    end.

The singer teetered dangerously but managed to recover his balance sufficiently to continue;

Just barely sixteen when he first came to fame
He blazed 'cross this county like a comet aflame
Until love threw its lasso and the Boy's heart was lost
Then cruel fate decreed just what this would cost . . .

That was as far as he got as gravity and John Barleycorn combined to get the upper hand. Still strumming, the troubadour tumbled off the stage backwards into the bar, upsetting a stack of empties which got the Chief all steamed up, which in turn convinced Jackson he should call it a night.

'You can hear the rest of your song next time round . . . next Saturday night if you're in town,' the proprietor reassured a protesting Turtle Ranch party and their girls as his burly bouncers ushered them to the door. 'That fool is always too ready to do that number just on account he wrote it. Thanks for coming, folks! Get the doors, boys.'

It was cold, dark and sobering in the echoing street. But this was as well for three revellers insofar as it jolted them back to reality. They weren't *really* freewheeling fiddle-foots any longer, the chill night proclaimed; hadn't really been ever since the day they'd caught that whiff of hangrope which could still bring on nightmares. They were cattlemen with responsibilities, their sobering expressions told one another sternly now. And if their lady-friends seemed more than a little put out when they realized they didn't even have time to escort them home, they were sure they'd get over it.

'Brrr!' Pike shivered as they swung into Maple and made for the dim night-light of the livery. 'Just what time is it anyway?'

Before Waco or Cassidy could take a guess, they found themselves passing by the shadowed front gallery of the hotel, bootheels rattling on worn planks. Suddenly a large shrouded figure reared up behind the railing and they caught the wicked glint of light on twin gun barrels.

'Judas Priest!' Pike yelled, backing up. 'What—?'

'Bail up!' the shotgunner yelled, but immediately lowered his ugly weapon as he found himself staring down at three youthful faces. 'Hell burn it, boys, I'm right sorry to skeer you thet way.' He booted his weapon and dragged off his hat. 'Goes to show just how jittery a man can git, don't it?'

'What the hell. . . !' Cassidy protested. 'You crazy or something, mister? Who'd you think we were?'

'I guess that ain't important.'

'It's important to us,' Pike retorted angrily. 'What's the game?'

The big man glanced over his shoulder at the darkened hotel, then frowned both ways along the shrouded street before replying.

'I guess it won't harm to tell you. The truth is, my boss here kinda parted on bad terms with the Fool Creekers 'way back when, and, well . . . I got the nighthawk keepin' watch jest in case they show up unexpected and ornery like. Savvy, lads?'

By this the partners had recovered some. They were still sore, but at least they understood.

'You might take a second look before you shove that thing in a man's face next time, pilgrim,' was all Pike said, and led the way for the livery and home.

It had been a long and exhausting visit to town. Suddenly they were dog-tired, the starlight was fading by the minute and the trail was long, cold and unfamiliar.

But naturally they raced all the long way home, which, if nothing else, proved they still had a way to go before they could rightly claim they'd really changed all that much.

The sprawling headquarters of Pawnee Ranch murmured busily under the south-western sun. Shadows flung by the huge hip-roofed barn and the stone-and-brick mansion fell gracefully upon carefully tended lawns, the wide gravel carriageway sweeping from the gate to the marble steps the warm color of ochre in the slant of the sun.

From a distance Judson Drake's headquarters appeared to be all show and glitter, but up close the impression was very different. From the gate could be heard the sharp clatter of pots and pans as the giant Chinese cook and his two best boys prepared the kind of chow to appeal to hard-working men who would come in off the range at dusk following a twelve-hour day expecting real food when they showed.

There was the sharp whistle of a boy summoning the milch cows punctuated by the angry tattoo of hoofs coming from the high-fenced breaking yards; the ring of hammer on steel from the forge and the background murmur of voices from the big sunfilled front room where Drake was holding council with his ramrod, straw-boss and bookkeeper.

'So, what am I expected to do about this?' Drake sounded as if he was seeking advice, but he wasn't. He was readying to make a statement. So nobody interrupted as he paused to torch a cigar into life and flick the dead match out the window.

The matter under consideration was a letter from someone – his staff didn't know who – requiring his immediate presence elsewhere. Normally when such mysterious missives reached Pawnee these days, Drake simply ordered his coach harnessed up, had Ash Pride muster two or three of the top guns and left, sometimes not to be sighted again for days on end.

Today he might have done the same thing but for two matters which seemed to demand his presence either here on the home acres or at the Pawnee office in Hardrock.

'How the devil can I leave when those fiddle-footed hicks are still occupying Mantrap and those jailhouse scum likely to show any minute? Answer me that.'

The three men present knew when to speak up and when to keep silent. They didn't offer a word.

'Times like this,' Drake continued, hands locked behind his back as he moved to the huge windows commanding a sweeping view of his kingdom, 'a man could be tempted to say the hell with all of them – the law, that toothless Citizens' Committee, public opinion and official censure – and just settle everything our own way and right now! Damned if he couldn't.' He whirled sharply. 'You understand what I'm saying?'

Three heads nodded. They knew right enough. They had seen him in this mood before, times that had led to violence and censure from the outside when Pawnee flexed its muscles and men felt the weight of Judson Drake's wrath.

'Er, mebbe . . . just mebbe, boss,' the gangling ramrod dared put in, 'Kelso won't come back. I mean, it's a week since they let the bunch outta Territory, and still no sign. Some figure he's had enough of the county, that he'll just keep travellin' until he finds someplace safe, which sure as shootin' ain't here.'

'Humph!'

Drake sounded dismissive but in truth was hopeful his man might be proven right. After all, it was five years since Pawnee and the Blind Fool Creek bunch had fought it out. Time enough for even a hothead like Kelso to forget threats made in the heat of the moment and realize they'd been lucky to escape with their lives, unlike Al Burke who'd been killed by Pawnee hands in the gunfight at One Eye Water.

But even if the Creekers might be written off it still left Turtle Ranch as a stumbling block.

He turned to his bookkeeper. 'You told the realtor I was prepared to double what those saddle-bums paid for Turtle?' The man nodded and Drake went on. 'So?'

'Waco, Cassidy and Pike said they aren't interested, Mr Drake. Sorry.'

'Your sympathy is both unwelcome and wasted, mister. What I want, what I will have, are results. Now do what you're paid for and get me what I want. All of you . . . out!'

In moments the most powerful man in Buffalo County

had the county's finest private room entirely to himself.

The urge for action clawed at Drake. His face was pale and his bleak eye lingered almost too long on the omnipresent silhouette of Ash Pride lounging on the shadowed front gallery, before he swung on his heel and strode through a polished mahogany doorway into the War Room.

This was his favorite part of the mansion. The high-walled library-cum-gentleman's lounge smelled richly of leather and waxed oak. There was a massive gray lime-stone fireplace with iron firedogs, and above, a pair of crossed flintlock rifles surmounted a lavish oil-painting of Valley Forge, where he claimed his grandfather had fought with great distinction.

His grandfather had been hanged for extortion in Missouri but Drake perpetuated the myth of his own creation. He was a highly successful man with a handsome wife and lovely daughter, who now craved status and acceptance as much as riches, goals made difficult by his innate ruthlessness which could surface at times and drive him to act more like an extortionist and murderer than dignified landed gentry.

He came to the War Room when in need of a calm atmosphere in which to think things through. Although he never read them, the bookcase with its set of Scott gleaming with gold tinting, the lithographs and mezzo-tints along the walls and the busts of Caesar and Lincoln helped to engender the reflective mood.

The dominant furnishing was a gleaming Queen Anne desk with locked drawers which held maps, documents and secrets to which only he had access.

Yet his treasured toys and trinkets did not have time to work their magic for him today before he realized he was not alone in his inner sanctum, and only one person would dare intrude here.

His daughter sat with her back to him on the black horsehair sofa, her hands clasped in her lap.

'Where are you going this time, father?' Her tone was impersonal and slightly critical. Arlena was perhaps the only person on God's earth who could get away with treating him as a mere mortal.

'I'm afraid you're mistaken, my dear,' he said, moving round the sofa to stand facing her. Despite his stature and advantages this large self-assured man often felt small and awkward in the presence of his own flesh and blood, for reasons both understood yet never discussed. 'I haven't yet decided if . . .'

'You're going off somewhere and it has something to do with Kelso, hasn't it?'

His smile was almost easy. She was way off the mark. True, the imminent return of the Creekers was never far from his thoughts these days, yet today's business had nothing to do with those jailbirds, he was happy to be able to truthfully insist.

'Business,' he declared ruefully. 'Just plain old boring business as usual, honey.'

'Why don't you ever confide in me, Father?'

'I'm confiding in you now.'

She rose, a tall and slender young woman who had adored her father once. But not now and never would she again.

'A moment ago you said you weren't going anywhere, now you say you are. Honestly, I don't know why I bother worrying about you, Father. Perhaps it's time I stopped.'

She swept from the impressive room signalling the abrupt end to yet another uneasy meeting between them,

71

which seemed to be almost the only kind they ever shared these days.

It took Drake some moments to recover his train of thought. He feared his daughter hated him now, and no degree of self-justification of past events could convince him she didn't have good reason.

He shook his head, drew deeply on his cigar and focused on the problem which had brought him here. He realized quickly he'd come half-way to a decision while speaking with the girl. His mind clearing swiftly now, he nodded to himself and confirmed that he knew what he must do; forget both Kelso and Turtle Ranch for the moment. Put the 'Operation' first, even if the presence of those 'aliens' remaining on the Turtle for much longer would surely adversely affect the prospects and future earnings of Drake Enterprises if allowed to go unchallenged.

Once made, the resolutions were promptly acted upon. By the time he quit the headquarters an hour later to go bowling along the well-graded road from the headquarters to the Hardrock trail under full escort, he knew his decision to be the right one.

Turtle Ranch and Kelso were small fish stacked up against the huge stakes he was playing for elsewhere, so he had totally convinced himself by the time they were on the north trail making for Hardrock. Tonight would see him handle some real big fish. He could get back to dealing with the tiddlers when that was done.

Judson Drake belonged to a breed almost unique to the West. Most often they were men who initially got to be successful cattlemen, eager and hungry to sweep up the range into their fists, men coming in from New Mexico or down from Kansas, big-moneyed and wide-ranging rogue bulls of the new time who craved to own a vast sweep of country and thirty thousand head of beef, as that had become the mark by which to measure a man in this frontier half of a nation.

And from ranching they went into importing and exporting, transport, railroading, banking, politics; into enterprises and schemes that could garner them honors and influence, and still greater power.

Drake already owned banks, business enterprises, shares and extensive mining interests along with vast additional slabs of real estate beyond the ranch which, like many of his interests, were largely secret. But it still wasn't enough, hence the Operation. The Operation was up north, and was his only interest important enough to have drawn him away at such an uncertain time in his affairs. It was so huge and exciting that if it succeeded as planned it might even appease his insatiable hunger for more and more of everything. Maybe.

The sun was well down as equipage and escort topped out a low timbered hill in the Dinosaurs overlooking Hardrock. The trail forked at the toe of the hill, one branch continuing on to the town, the other bypassing it by a mile to the west.

They took the bypass trail and by sundown were many miles to the north travelling through increasingly rugged country marked by stands of gaunt timber and gouged viciously by deep arroyos and gullywashes, which eventually made coach travel impossible. At that point Drake and four men continued on horseback leaving two behind with the coach.

It was rough going but Drake was an accomplished and hardy horseman. He felt relaxed enough to be able to study his surrounds with lusty eagerness, envisioning what this hard scrabble country could deliver him if he just kept his nerve and maintained secrecy.

He was looking at a degenerated landscape peopled by gaunt and gray trees while envisioning something far different and exciting. He swallowed as he ducked beneath a reaching limb. He'd gambled all his life, he reflected. But this time he was gambling big time. In reality he was risking just about all he possessed on just one huge roll of the dice.

There was still a little light left when the party came to a battered old fence and gate situated in the middle of noplace. This was as far as the full escort went; the southern boundary of Big T Ranch. Ash Pride alone accompanied his employer beyond that gate, the others dismounting to await their return, however long that might be.

Before full darkdown the two riders got to see the brooding, crouched beast of Spur Range off to their left, but there was nothing but dry grasslands and stunted vegetation where they rode. Big T Ranch ran acres to the cow, not cows to the acre. The soil here was sour, water scarce and wolves found it an attractive retreat from hunters' guns elsewhere. Even so, right now Judson Drake found it infinitely more attractive than even the lush spring greenery and all his fattening Hereford herds of Pawnee.

'There's the mile marker, boss,' said Pride, breaking a long silence as they passed a white-painted stump in the night. 'Not far now.'

The tycoon just grunted and concentrated on following the faint trace of trail beneath the ghostly starlight. As they splashed across a shallow creek the silence was suddenly broken by the sound of a low distant wailing some distance ahead. It was the unmistakable sound of a train in the night, yet the nearest railroad lay more than thirty miles north.

6
Big Men and Bad

On a day destined to witness several seemingly discon-
nected events that would forever change the course of
Buffalo County history, a blood-red sunrise, all ominous
and threatening, might have seemed more in keeping.
Instead, first light crept timidly into the eastern skies
above Flint Peak to send soft streamers of pink and gold
out across the big land to alert all the innocent sleepers
that a new day had begun.

The night-cold in the high country still lingered, fresh
and sweet. But far out across the northern plains where
the coyotes called and coveys of quail burst abruptly out of
the long grasses, the new daylight was turning railroad
tracks to gleaming pewter as the Cannonball Special came
clanging and clashing into the tiny rickety siding with a
racket to wake the dead.

'All out fer Olan's Siding!' bawled the mustachioed
depotmaster, as though his station was something really
important and not just a tiny flyspeck of life in the vast
stretch of grass and sage. A mighty billow of steam erupted
from the fifty-ton Titan loco to engulf his swaybacked

figure in dusty navy blue, and when it finally cleared he was no longer alone on his narrow little strip of carefully tended Company territory.

He had company.

Standing squat and stolid by the rusting water-tank in back of him now was a stranger, while directly before him momentarily poised motionless on the steel steps of the green-painted Pullman car, stood five hard-faced men whose manner was both intimidating yet remote.

The depotmaster gave ground and Kelso's boots hit Buffalo County dirt for the first time in five years. Without a word the tall, hard-bodied figure stepped lithely by him to grip the hand of Lucius Brown. A former fellow inmate of Territory, Brown currently occupied the role of advance agent and fringe friend to the former rakehell bunch of country boys known only down south as the Blind Fool Creek outfit, or Creekers.

In turn the others greeted Brown, who then led them round in back of the unpainted ticket office where their saddle horses stood tied up, swishing flies.

They were mounting up before the uneasy depotmaster remembered his duty and belatedly blew his whistle to set the train heading eastwards again.

As loco, car, tender and boxcar quickly gathered speed, the horsemen deliberately cut across the tracks barely feet in front of the cowcatcher. Without a backwards glance the party went storming away southwards at full gallop to leave the man in dusty navy all alone. And reflecting on whom he'd just seen, the man was more than happy to be that way.

That same sun was two hours into the sky when Marshal Dalton rode back into Hardrock on his brown mare. As he cut onto the main street by the general store he found himself automatically scanning the plankwalks for signs of new arrivals during his absence, didn't know if he should feel relieved or anxious when he sighted none.

Over recent days it had become the lawman's habit to rise early and conduct a horse-patrol of the town's surrounds before 'most anybody was up and about. He would not admit he was looking for first sign of the Blind Fool Creek party, for to have done so would be to admit he was anxious and that was no way for a good peace officer to operate.

Things had been relatively peaceful for the lawman until he'd received that warning wire from the warden of Territory. Since then a climate of unease had engulfed his town as citizens waited nervously to see what Dalton and Judson Drake would do should Kelso come back looking for vengeance for what had happened that day in the courthouse next door to the law office.

There was still debate over that case five years on. Had Kelso and his pards from the creek really gone after Drake in retaliation for the big man's attempts to force them off their place, which was now part of Pawnee Ranch? Or had it been the other way round; an attack by Drake to rid himself of a troublesome bunch once and for all?

Likely nobody would ever be sure, and in truth the marshal no longer much cared. The Pawnee–Blind Fool Creek shootout was history now. What signified was what might happen here and now if they should rise one morning to sight the ex-cons loping in over the buffalo-grass plains.

The marshal sighed and steered his horse into the jail-house. Stepping down stiffly, he tied up and glanced around. The hotel roustabout was sweeping the boardwalk out front without much enthusiasm, and he remembered that Drake had bought the hotel lock stock and barrel just last week, along with the adjoining stage depot where a mud-stained Concord coach was visible in back with a hostler guiding a wheeler into the harness. Another ordinary day in his town – or should that be Drake's town now – coming up, he could only hope.

He found mail on his desk when he went inside. He sat scanning the regular information sheet from Head Office detailing recent crimes, court cases and the like which all lawmen should know about, and thus was made familiar with the court case involving the new men up at Mantrap Valley, Waco, Cassidy and Pike.

Dalton nodded slowly as he read. The documentation stated that those youngsters had had a close call up north but had been completely cleared. For some reason he felt good about that; that trio was like a big blast of fresh air in his too-tense town. Still, just thinking about them raised yet another problem. Drake wanted the Turtle Ranch, God alone knew why. Could be trouble out there as well as in town, with the big man whom he secretly feared involved in both. Naturally.

He glanced up at the spidery hands of the Seth Thomas clock on the wall. Too early for an early shot? Maybe not.

Noontime sunlight shimmered upon the gleaming gold roof of the luxury railroad car drawn up at a hidden siding in the Dinosaur Hills twenty miles north, where Judson Drake held the floor. Surrounded by silver-haired railroad tycoons with fat cigars and bristling mustaches, the cattleman who aspired to become so much more was painting a glowing picture of the immediate future as it would affect them all including the grizzled boss of the Big T Ranch upon whose land tracks, luxury car and brass-trimmed locomotive stood.

His business partners needed some reassuring at this point of time and Drake was able to give it to them. He had quietly bought up better than half the property and land available in Hardrock over the past month, he informed them smugly, and was talking huge future profits enthusiastically and convincingly as fresh Cubans were set alight and silent waiters in livery topped up ice-clinking crystal glasses. Just a short distance away sweating gangs of blue-garbed tracklayers were slogging away at the serious business of laying another length of track pointing due south.

Ash Pride leaned against the scrolled-iron observation platform of the splendid car with a cigarette jutting from between his lips, watching everything and missing nothing. What was taking place on the Big T was not illegal by any means but it was covert for business reasons and must remain so until his employer solved certain major problems back home, namely the Creekers' imminent return, and those bums out on Turtle Ranch.

Pride's pale eyes glittered.

He was looking forward to both challenges, and in a habitual unconscious action hitched up the double gunrig buckled round narrow hips as he took another stroll along the right of way past the car. From what he could overhear, Mr Drake was still holding the floor in there.

Mid-afternoon sun smiled down upon Chief Long Bear as he hauled the fat silver fish from the river and removed the hook. His actions were deliberate and sure and he didn't need to look at his fingers to know what they were doing.

This was the Chief's special time of day when he made his stately way from the saloon down to the river bank. Here noontimes he could be alone with his thoughts away from the ceaseless activity of his place of business, reflect on the past and commune with the spirits of his people and often with that of the Boy.

The Chief always fished alone. The only time this had been different had been when Jimmy Kaine would accompany him down to the river any old time he pleased. It had seemed an oddly matched friendship between a full-blooded Choctaw Indian and the kid who'd drifted in and out of the lives of so many so memorably back in what the Chief always thought of as the great days. But they were close. And the day the boy drowned in this very river remained one of the darkest in the life of this wise man who'd seen so much of violence and tragedy in the West he loved so much.

The Chief smiled as he turned to head back, fishing pole over his shoulder, moving with the sure-footed pigeon-toed gait of his race. Strange these days; whenever he got to think about Jimmy those youngsters from Turtle kept intruding on his mind. Shouldn't surprise him, he reflected, for surely all four of them were cracked from the same mould. That thought made him feel pretty good as he strolled back through a town still very much on tenterhooks about Kelso's return.

For himself, the Chief never worried about things like that. He'd always gotten along fine with the Blind Fool Creekers, troublesome as they were. And even if this had not been the case he still wouldn't be concerned about their coming home. It was a white man's way, to fret and worry. It had taken him a lifetime to achieve serenity and it shielded him like chain-mail.

Late afternoon sunlight flooded Turtle Creek as the workers paused to survey what had been accomplished. They'd patched the worst hole in the ranch-house roof but had run out of nails before they could finish replacing the veranda planking. Somebody was going to have to go to town at the weekend for more supplies, it was agreed, but when it came to deciding on just who should go was when the wrangling started.

Trouble was, they liked it in town. They were doing just fine out here, they reasoned, but wondered if maybe they couldn't go a little easier on themselves regarding restricting visits to Hardrock. No reason they should be scared of civilization and its temptations just because of what had happened up north, so they assured each other. They were now respectable citizens of Buffalo County and should be able to rely upon themselves to act as such.

They were feeling much better by the time they'd brewed some joe, and drew lots to see who would ride nighthawk and who would handle the chore of looking for more wild stuff they'd heard about tomorrow.

It was a magic time of day as the sun was swallowed by the hills and the big longhorn bull came mooching across to the house looking for a handout. They sat on the stoop talking and smoking, and there was little left but an aura of dying light outlining the mesa when they suddenly fell silent, staring upwards.

Silhouetted against the pale golden haze was the figure of a horseman, motionless but for the breeze stirring the animal's mane and tail. The slender rider was staring down into the valley. Leastways that was how it seemed as they came to their feet to stare back, only to realize the mesa crest was now empty.

'What the tarnation?' Waco breathed. 'Where'd he go?'

'Never mind that. Who was he?' queried Pike. 'Nobody wanders about up here to hell and gone.'

'Know what,' Cassidy said slowly. 'I reckon it must have been like a mirage. You know, when you think you see something but you really don't . . .'

They continued to stare. There was nothing there, and soon the mesa was engulfed by the night. They looked at one another in silence, and then Pike mentioned food which triggered off another heated debate on whether they'd have beans or beef for supper . . . at the silvery end of just another day in Buffalo County.

Abe Cassidy worked his way upwards through drizzling veils of rain. As the rain thinned, he glanced back down over the crouching monster of the mesa to see Mantrap Valley looking small and snug far below. Smoke curled lazily from the chimney. He thought he could make out activity at the corrals but wasn't sure at this range. He'd not left a note. They'd been visited by the rancher from a neighboring spread who'd told where they might find some 'Freeze-Up stuff' if they were desperate enough to go looking for it.

He was going looking and was doing it alone. No way those two wouldn't have insisted on accompanying him had they known his intentions. One man was all they could afford to spare today in the ongoing hunt for more wild cattle up in the chilly Bearclaws region of the Comanche Hills. Their 'herd' had busted down a section of rickety fence overnight and both Pike and Waco were better hands with hammers, clippers and wire than himself, or at least so it suited him to attest.

He grinned at the thought, then concentrated on the trail, a prudent habit when riding these lofty ridges. No sign of cattle yet; no sign of any life for that matter.

The cattle Cassidy was searching for were a different

83

breed from the small bunch they'd already acquired. They were the descendants of the original stock that had reached the barricade of the Comanches in great drifts a decade earlier following what the Midwest still referred to as the Freeze-Ups. The name identified the two successive winters which exceeded in severity anything within even Indian memory. Ferocious blizzards had come raging down out of the Great Divide choking Wyoming, Colorado and New Mexico with snow and ice for months on end.

Back in those early days, the ranchers were still battling Indians, disease and a myriad of other hardships, and few had time or money to expend on fences.

As a result, as the buffalo had done since time immemorial when such freak weather struck, the range cattle headed instinctively southwards. There was no stopping them. Many a man lost his entire herd while he huddled helpless and snowbound in his cabin. Their loss had been Buffalo County's gain, even if only a tiny proportion of the migrating herds survived the Freeze-Ups. Those which did were eagerly rounded up and formed the basis of many a successful southern rancher's fortune.

Their cowman neighbor insisted there were still descendants of the disaster to be found in the Bearclaws, 'Iffen a man's desperate enough to go look.'

Cassidy wasn't desperate, just ambitious and energetic. Enough so that by noon with the weather finally lifting he'd put three lofty plateaux behind him and had his sights set on a beckoning rock-walled basin higher up, when glancing back down through a gap in the timber he sighted the horsemen.

He reined in sharply.

Two men stood by their horses a mile below upon a gray slab of stone jutting out of the mountainside which

84

commanded a full view of Mantrap Valley. Watery sunlight glinted off something metallic. His mind flashed back to the sniper, until he realized one was using field-glasses. He plucked his own set from a saddle-bag and set them to his eyes. The men jumped into sharp focus; a blocky fellow in a yellow slicker and a leaner figure with the glasses who appeared somehow familiar.

The nickel dropped when the latter turned and he recognized him as the Pawnee Ranch man who'd been with Ash Pride at the Greasy Spoon.

So what were Pawnee hands doing up here, obviously spying on the Turtle? It couldn't be anything good.

Immediately he started down. This was free range and they had no right to move anyone on. But he would claim the right to at least find out what Drake men were doing this far from home, watching their land.

He was closing in through the timber when the chestnut dislodged a rock, which rolled off the trail and dropped noisily into a stony gulch. Instantly he heard hoofbeats and by the time he had the lookout slab in sight again it was empty.

He rode on down and reined in to slide out of his saddle. Cigarette butts indicated the men had been there some time. He scowled and massaged the back of his neck. They didn't discuss Judson Drake and his interest in the Turtle much. But in their time here they'd formed a clear picture of the cattle baron as the breed who always got what he wanted and wasn't too particular how he went about it.

Rolling a cigarette, he set it alight, swung back up and was sitting his saddle considering whether to report what had happened below or continue his search, when he heard the distant sound of Goober's barking.

His gaze cut back to the spread to see a rider crossing their graze by one of their ponds with Waco and Pike watching from the yards.

This supposedly remote piece of cow country was getting crowded!

He took up the glasses again and focused on the newcomer. His jaw sagged in surprise. The rider was female, and even at this distance it was all too plain she was as handsome a woman as he'd sighted since hitting the county. Even Goober's barking sounded excited.

He didn't tarry. He headed downtrail fast. . . .

7

Drake's Daughter

Arlena Drake was beautiful. She had raven hair with blue glints in it. Her skin was pale and and her eyes were dark blue with velvet irises. In her tailored riding clothes, tan calf-boots and a fashionable little hat perched on the back of her head she might have sat for a photograph in a fashion magazine but for her manner. This girl, whom a trio of deeply impressed new ranchers were already rating as likely the first genuine beauty they'd glimpsed since coming south, was no easy smiling heartbreaker but rather appeared serious bordering on somber in a manner far beyond her years.

Which didn't deter them one iota, or even come close to stopping them from competing to outdo one another in welcoming hospitality as they ushered their visitor inside and shot each other dark and threatening looks behind her back. 'Mine!' each glare pronounced. And it was like they were back along Raccoon Creek, too young for the War, too old for school, dreaming only of 'their'

West and all the impossibly wonderful women they'd meet out there one day.

'Coffee, ma'am, er, miss . . . or can we call you Arlena, mebbe?' Waco fussed, assisting her remove her nifty riding-hat.

She almost smiled, this regal creature, as she gazed from one eager face to another. 'Arlena will do fine,' she said. 'And you are . . . Clem, Abe and Luke. Do I have it right now? And yes, coffee would be lovely.'

By the time they'd fixed coffee and dug out some on-the-turn cracker biscuits from somewhere, they were beginning to relax and act more normally, while their quick exchange of glances asked the same question. What was Judson Drake's daughter doing to hell and gone out here visiting with them? They certainly weren't complaining, but a man just had to be deeply curious, maybe even wary.

Crossing one long leg over another, the visitor sipped her coffee and prudently declined a cracker. She glanced round the room, at the battered furnishings, the papered-over side window, the breakfast crockery still stacked in the wash dish. They hoped she noticed everything was clean if none too flash.

Then she said easily, 'I'm very impressed. I rather thought I would be.'

'Huh?' Pike was not the articulate one. But he managed to add, 'Impressed with what, miss . . . er, Arlena?' He managed a grin. 'The spread or us?'

'Oh, I've seen Turtle Ranch before,' she replied. 'I used to come riding out here . . .' A momentary pause; 'With Jimmy . . .'

That rang a bell.

Whether a man solicited them or not, in Buffalo County

Where Legends Ride

Jimmy Kaine stories were almost impossible to avoid. it was 'Jimmy did this . . . Jimmy used to say that . . .' until you could get a little weary of it. Naturally a man expected to hear such yarns around the saloons where apparently 'The Boy' had been no stranger 'way back when. The percentage girl with a skinful, the man you bought your supplies from in town, and even Hardrock's own preacherman had all laid their own favorite Jimmy tale on the newcomers by this. They were interested, of course, but not overly so. They were too busy living their own challenging lives in the big country to pay more than cursory interest to figures from the past, colorful though they might be.

None the less they were always polite where pretty women were involved. So easy-smiling Waco said, 'We hear tell Kaine was a friend of yours, Miss Arlene?'

'Please . . . just Arlena, Clem.' Her eyes drifted to the front window, and Cassidy wished he'd given it a bit of a shine with the elbow when he was tidying up. 'Yes, we were friends.' A shrug. 'But then again, Jimmy was friends with nearly everyone.'

'Except your father,' Pike drawled, drawing a warning frown from Cassidy who stood leaning against the mantel.

'My goodness, you do seem to have learned a great deal in a relatively short time, don't you?'

Arlena Drake's voice carried a clipped Eastern inflection. She had been educated in Boston, extensively and expensively. Her father had groomed her to become a glittering aristocratic princess destined to one day make a brilliant and advantageous marriage. Instead she had taken up with a reckless youth who'd become some sort of legend for many of the wrong reasons.

'So you were . . . good friends?' persisted Pike, feeding his dog chittling bits from a coffee tin.

89

'You're no doubt wondering what on earth I'm doing here?' she countered, deftly shifting the subject. 'It's quite simple really. I heard about you, you sounded rather nice – which I suspect now might well be the case and I felt a duty to ride up and, well, warn you, I suppose.'

She'd captured their interest from the outset. This interest was heightened now as they studied her closely.

' 'Bout what?' Waco was blunt.

'My father, of course.' She rose and moved towards the doorway to gaze out. 'I know you came by this place legitimately by somehow beating father to the punch. But you should not imagine for a moment that that is the end of the matter. For some reason which I can't imagine, he has set his heart on acquiring Turtle Ranch and I know positively that he has no intention of allowing you to remain here. You have no idea how furious he was the day he returned home from the auction empty-handed.'

She turned to face them.

'I want you to sell out to him. He will pay you well, I'm sure of that. More than enough to buy a better place somewhere not so isolated and difficult perhaps.'

Silence fell.

Three sober men were studying the young woman and sharing but a single thought; had Drake deputized his daughter to act on his behalf to get what he wanted?

Hands on hips, Waco stood before her and put their suspicion into words. She smiled faintly, wearily it would seem.

'Of course you'd have to think that way, Clem, all of you. But, no, my father cannot coerce or even persuade me to do very much of anything ever since ... well, I'm sure by now you've heard of what happened? With Jimmy and me, I mean?'

'Something about this Kaine feller tangling with your daddy and getting drownded in Silver River, wasn't it?' said Pike.

She nodded. 'In any event, all that's of no importance now.' Again she met the eyes of all three in turn. 'But I do want you to promise you'll at least take my warning seriously. What father wants, father gets. I can't put it any more simply than that. I'd hate to have anything nasty happen out here and know I might have prevented it.' She reached for her hat. 'Well, I thank you gentlemen for your hospitality, and now I must be going—'

'There were two Pawnee men spying on us just before you arrived,' Cassidy broke in abruptly. Up until then he'd scarcely spoken. There was good reason for this. He was entranced by this girl's dark beauty, her air almost of melancholy; her every gesture, movement and word which seemed to invoke a world and way of life almost unimaginable to a poorboy drifter from Raccoon Creek, Tennessee.

The girl looked suddenly pale. 'Are you sure, Al?'

'That's Abe. Yeah, I'm dead sure. They took off fast when they heard me coming.' He paused, considered mentioning the shooting incident, decided against it. 'Any notion why they'd be out here, Arlena?'

She shook her head, blue-black hair making a soft rustling sound upon her shoulders. She bit her underlip, like she might be about to cry.

'I don't know what is going on anymore,' she said unevenly. 'Father's away so much these days. And he's hardly slept since learning the Blind Fool Creek men were released from prison. He's hired extra gunhands, and I overheard him telling Ash Pride he was prepared to use all force necessary to protect himself if those men should

91

prove troublesome again. Added to all this he's even more involved in business than ever at the moment. He has all sorts of important people coming and going day and night. I know him well enough to know he's working on some big project, perhaps even something huge. Whenever he's in this mode I know from experience that people will end up getting hurt. He . . . he doesn't seem to care about that anymore, I'm afraid. And now I really must go before it gets dark.'

She hurried out to the tooth-gnawed tie rack, leaving them staring after her. Waco was first to reach for his flat-brim. 'We can't let a lady go lone-ridin' all the way back down to the plains.'

'The man's right, you know,' Luke Pike said to Cassidy as Goober led the eager way out. 'Everything's secure here, I even fed the chickens . . .'

'Hell, you don't have to convince me what we've got to do, bucko,' Cassidy protested, and beat him to the door.

The moon was peering over the mighty shoulder of Mount Ratenal by the time the party finally left the Comanche foothills behind them. Riding alongside Arlena Drake, Cassidy was startled to see the lights of Hardrock reflecting from a low bank of cloud just about a mile ahead. The cattle king's daughter had insisted on showing them a short cut, to the Pawnee, but by his calculations the spread lay several miles due west of this point.

He looked a quick question at her, was surprised to see her smile. She wasn't much for smiling, but then maybe she didn't have a lot to smile about.

'You're right, I've deceived you,' she confessed. 'But it's such a lovely night that I thought . . .' She paused to glance back at the others. 'I thought you might like to see something interesting. Of course, if you'd rather escort me straight home . . .'

'No, something interesting sounds, well, real interesting,' said Pike.

'I'm *always* interested in something interesting,' affirmed Waco, quick grin flashing.

Cassidy chuckled. They were eager for diversion, he knew. Like himself They'd slogged like grade-layers all week long. They'd walked, talked and breathed nothing but work. But offered any excuse to escape it all and grab a quick taste of something light and different, well, there was still enough Raccoon Creek in their blood to guarantee they would seize that opportunity 'most every time.

He nodded assent and the girl led them off across an open mile of sweet grass and nodding bluebonnets to a shallow fording. They crossed then kept on across country towards the lights until a squat low hill bulked before them.

'Mount Oakey,' Arlena supplied perfunctorily, and they followed her up along the tracery of a twisting road, ghostly and faint in the moonlight.

As they neared the crest Goober started in sniffing about suspiciously, and when the partners sighted a canting wooden headboard atop the grassy crest, all looked sharply at their guide. Arlena seemed serenely unaware of their reaction as she guided her Arab mare between several neglected graves before reining in and stepping down.

'Here,' she gestured, indicating a drab gravesite marked by a simple headboard at the base of which stood a glass bowl filled with fresh-looking flowers. 'This is something I wanted you to see tonight . . . that I felt you should . . .'

Her voice trailed away. The three dismounted and stood in a line staring at the grave. The inscription on the plain wooden marker was clearly legible in the moonlight. It read;

HERE LIES HENRY DOOLIN

1825–1876

R.I.P.

If Doolin had lived a significant or distinguished life in Buffalo County, none of this was reflected in his final resting place. No suggestion of romance, mystery or magic haunted this desolate boot hill where a vagrant nightwind stirred drooping sycamores and scruboaks trembling the stem of a puny cedar sapling planted just a few paces from the gravesite. There was a brief puzzled silence before the girl spoke again.

'Mr Doolin was a family friend and a supplier of timber to our mill in town. Some time ago he and father became involved in a dispute over money up at the Doolins' place on Crow Ridge in which Mr Doolin was shot and killed. Jimmy Kaine was there also, as he was a close friend of the Doolins. He fled following the shooting. When he finally showed in town several days later the marshal arrested him and charged him with the murder. Jimmy protested his innocence. But the judge influenced the jury to bring in a guilty verdict. He escaped the same night and has been a fugitive ever since.'

'Did he do it?' Waco asked bluntly.

'No.' She sounded sure. 'I don't know who shot Mr Doolin, only that it wasn't Jimmy.' She touched a square of lace to her eyes. 'Jimmy brought me here several times,' she said with controlled emotion. 'He made me promise to have him buried here amongst what he always refers to as "his" people, meaning the poor and the exploited. He . . . he has always believed he will die young.'

Cassidy studied her closely before daring to say, 'We've heard a whole heap about this Jimmy Kaine – can't help it here, I guess. Of course folks have told us that you and him are, well, you know. . . ?'

Arlena now appeared calmer as she bent to brush dead grass away from the cedar sapling. 'That is one thing rich and poor have in common I suppose – a tendency to talk too much.' There was no reading her expression as she straightened, fingering the small leaves of the cedar. 'Gossip has had me running off to New Mexico with Jimmy a dozen times in the past. Of course the same applies to most of the other young men I know. But I believe they like the notion of coupling me with Jimmy best because it makes for more exciting gossip . . . me, Judson Drake's daughter, and Jimmy supposedly so wild and even dangerous, or so some would have you believe . . .'

Her words trailed off. Luke Pike dared ask, 'Then you and Kaine were, like, a-courtin', Miss Arlena?'

But she seemed not to hear as she indicated the baby cedar.

'I planted this for Mr Doolin. Father refused to permit me to erect a headstone or anything like that. That was cruel of him, for the Doolins loved me and often minded me as a child. I suspect he resented the fact that Ma and Pa Doolin were also close to Jimmy and regarded him as a hero as he is to so many, including me I suspect. You see, he loves Buffalo County and I've lost count of the times he helped people out, risked his life for friends, or stood up to dangerous and powerful people – such as my father –

on behalf of someone unable to help themselves.'

She broke off abruptly, finding three sober young men staring at her curiously. She flushed and dropped her eyes to her hands.

'I'm sorry. I know I tend to carry on about Jimmy at times.'

They nodded as though they now understood about Arlena Drake and Jimmy the Boy.

'Hell of a lot of folks do that,' Cassidy said. 'Boost Jimmy Kaine, that is. We're kind of sorry we missed him.'

'You would like him,' she said simply. 'For you men really are very like him in so many ways. And he would like you – wouldn't you Jimmy?'

A vague unease touched them at this, for she seemed to be speaking to the night. They found the nocturnal atmosphere of the rude graveyard – apparently reserved for ne'er-do-wells, of one stripe or another – almost palpable. This whole event appealed to their quirky natures. But when anybody, even someone as magnetically attractive as Arlena Drake, got to holding conversations with absent company, it was plainly time to break camp.

The ride across to the Pawnee was uneventful. The nighthawk patrols had been doubled and in some areas trebled since the release of Kelso and the Creekers. But Arlena knew where the security was strong and where weak, and was able to lead them skilfully and safely through woods, meadows and grazing lands to reach a grassy plateau where sleeping red cattle dreamed in clusters, her gesture inviting them to take in their first glimpse of the brilliantly torchlit castle of Judson Drake's grass kingdom.

They were impressed. They had to be. To brag they'd bested the county's wealthiest man was one thing, but to see and feel the full material importance and dimensions of that adversary was almost intimidating. Naturally they tried to hide it.

'Wouldn't trade your home for mine, girl,' Waco joked. 'What must you pay in *taxes?*'

She smiled. Her melancholy appeared to have lifted.

Then Pike asked curiously, 'Your daddy always have the place lighted up like a country fairground this way?'

She sobered. 'Not until recently.' She seemed tense. 'I'm afraid all this is connected to the release of the Blind Fool Creek boys. Everything lit up, extra gunhands, father barely sleeping . . . all of it. I'm afraid it will go on like this until we know what's going to happen when . . . when Kelso comes home. . . .'

Cassidy cleared his throat. 'Reckon you could find yourself be in danger when that happens?'

'I think not.' She nodded as if to emphasize her own thoughts. 'Indeed, I never considered the Blind Fool Creek boys half as bad as they were painted. I'm sure things will work out.'

'You could call on us if there was need,' Cassidy insisted.

'You're very sweet. You all are. Yes, I know I shouldn't say that to men I've barely met. But I do feel we get along very well, don't you? And I find I'm now in full agreement with the Chief who insists you are so much like Jimmy, each one of you. It was very kind of you to see me safely home.' Her eyes lingered on Cassidy momentarily, or so he wanted to believe. 'Goodnight, and do take care and consider what I asked you to do about your ranch, please. . . .'

Then she was gone on the white-socked black mare, slender and straight-backed in her custom-built Spanish-Texan saddle.

'Poor little rich girl, huh,' Pike murmured sympathetically. 'Mean old daddy, and her stuck on a wanted killer.'

'She didn't say she was sweet on Kaine,' Cassidy said quickly, maybe too quickly.

She sure as shootin' didn't say she *wasn't*,' Waco remarked drily.

'Well, for mine I'm about up to here with what a nonesuch wonder that geezer's supposed to be.' Pike was acerbic. Then he added, 'Damn sure she's too good for him anyways. Mebbe too classy for any poor boy . . .'

The smaller Arlena Drake's receding figure became the more noticeably did harsh reality seem to come crowding in upon the watchers from the plateau. She had buoyed them along. Only now did they grow aware that the night was quite cold and they were dog-weary from the brutal week they'd had. There was a sense of anticlimax as they turned the muddy roan, short-tailed chestnut and bottle-nosed dun back along the same safe route they'd followed in.

What now – now that reality was back?

Luke Pike pondered this for a full half-mile before suddenly breaking the silence. 'I love my granny.'

Cassidy and Waco stared at him. 'Granny Green?' the latter quizzed with a frown; they often quoted irascible Granny Green from their Raccoon Creek days.

'Granny Pike back home in Hogback, Tennessee,' Pike corrected.

'What the hell's your granny got to do with anything?' Cassidy was irritable. He would have liked to spend the whole night riding round the countryside with Drake's daughter.

'Well, like I say, I love her,' Pike replied. Then he almost shouted, 'But right now I'd sell her into slavery for a double rye whiskey, b'God!'

Dotted strategically across the Pawnee's moon-blue acres, jittery, gunpacking nighthawks pricked their ears at the sudden stutter of galloping horses. Sounded like someone heading for town.

Molita was the Mexican who operated the dry-goods store where they bought their supplies. Over a late beer with the man at the Chief's he happened to mention a gander which they showed interest in, so he invited them back to his place to see it. Cassidy, Waco and Pike trooped into the meticulously clean little adobe, and there he was, smiling life-sized at them from a gilt frame above the mantel in that easy way he had, cigarette jutting from between his teeth and that banner of yellow hair tumbled carelessly across his brow.

The drifter.

'Who's this?' Pike blinked.

'Why, Jimmy Kaine, of course, *amigos*. Why do you seem so surprised? Every second Mexican house in Buffalo County boasts its own picture of Jimmy the Boy.'

They didn't reveal their interest in or contact with a man on the run; couldn't think of more than one or maybe two people they might confide in. But before they left and without the gander – they learned that Kaine was venerated amongst the Mexicans of Hardrock for having once saved one of their children from a runaway horse.

On the street again, three wondering Kentuckians scowled at one another, scratched their heads and tried to figure firstly how come they hadn't got to guess at a connection between the widely admired Jimmy the Boy and their drifter. And the second puzzle; why did a man running from a hangrope appear willing to take such hair-raising risks just to help them out?

'Simple,' declared their confidant the Chief over a late nightcap in his backyard patio. 'You boys bucked Drake, which Jimmy knows better than anybody puts you in real danger, so he does whatever he can to at least give you a fighting chance.'

'But . . . but do folks know he's still hanging around hereabouts?' a mystified Cassidy wanted to know.

'They know Jimmy Kaine would never quit Buffalo County.'

'Someone'll run him up a rope if he keeps chancin' his arm,' predicted Waco. 'I'd be in Mexico, in his boots.'

'He'll never go,' sighed the Chief. He looked from one face to the other. 'I believe he's hoping you boys won't either. Could be he feels we need your breed here.'

Waco, Cassidy and Pike stared back at the big bronzed man in silence, feeling the sudden weight of new responsibility. The strange thing was that it seemed to feel good.

8

When Kelso
Came to Town

Bishop, Nathan, Longhorn and Cleal trailed Kelso and Brown up into Hardrock from the river. As the horsemen approached Maple Street they could feel the tension preceding them like electricity running ahead of a summer storm. With the exception of their leader, the bunch of former Blind Fool Creek riders were tense and watchful as they sat more erect in their saddles hands feeling stiff on the reins, weak sunlight shimmering on bridle metal and gun handles.

This was a day five years coming.

Kelso alone appeared relaxed, exactly as Hardrock remembered him. Whether this was really the case or otherwise was anybody's guess. Hardrock had been on tenterhooks waiting for the bunch's return for more than a week, and although nobody had ever expected them to just show up like this in broad daylight, there was a kind of relief underlying their anxiety as Kelso pushed his horse slightly ahead of Brown's to be first into the broad main street.

At last the waiting and uncertainty was over. And perhaps this was a good sign; Kelso just leading his boys in like this just like in the old days instead of maybe trying to torch Pawnee Ranch and Hardrock or whatever an angry man might choose to settle old scores.

'Kel' Kelso didn't look markedly different from the day he was led away in chains five years back. This was the initial impression shared by passers-by, storekeepers, porch-loungers and women armed with shopping baskets with kids in tow along the western end of the street as the clip-clop of shod hoofs filled the sudden quiet.

Yet this vaguely reassuring feeling only survived as long as it took for the riders to draw abreast when Kelso's stare sought them out from beneath the shadow of his hat brim. The impact of that flat stare struck even old acquaintances like a physical blow; a glint of winter sunlight glancing directly off Kilgore's Glacier couldn't have been chillier. And seeing this, every silent citizen knew one thing for sure. The horrors of Territory Penitentiary had not broken this man they'd once known well, nor had it reformed him. Kelso had fought his captors every inch and every second, and it showed.

'So, what you reckon, Kel?' Brown hissed, bringing his horse's Roman nose abreast of the leader's stirrup. 'Is this like you expected, or what?'

Brown was scum. He was a bitter loser who'd hitched his wagon to Kelso's star in the pen and had been rewarded with honorary membership in the bunch. Thus far, he'd done his job well enough. But this scary 'Sunday parade' style of entering Hardrock found him wanting. He would readily garrotte a blind man in a back alley in the dark with every advantage his way, but this display of bravado sent hot knives lancing through his bowels.

'Shut up and sit straight!' Kelso retorted as they passed the Main Street Flophouse to approach Charlie's Greasy Spoon. He snapped his fingers just once and both Bishop and Nathan overtook a white-faced Brown and drew abreast. 'Watch the roofs and parapets,' he warned softly. 'If you see one damn thing, shoot first and find out what it was later. Pass the word!'

To the watchers from the Three Deuces, the hotel, Lil's place and Jackson's Dining Rooms, it appeared as though the riders were just chatting amongst themselves as Buck Bishop fell back to speak with Longhorn and Cleal, while Kelso made an aside to a prison-pale Cleat Nathan.

These onlookers might also have been deceived that it all seemed pretty much like the old days when the Blind Fool Creekers had come to town to howl at the moon, trigger off saloon brawls and bad-mouth Judson for trying to force them off the run-down spread Kelso had inherited from his no-account daddy . . . but for that tingle down the spine they got whenever they studied the leader of the pack.

Kelso was tall and slim, yet, you sensed, strong. He favored his late father in appearance, physique and the way he sat a horse. He was hard as a whipstock, with bits of sharp steel for eyes. He'd always looked a tough one, now he appeared downright dangerous. A wise man had said once that he regarded Kelso as the universal soldier, disciplined, aggressive, hard-bodied and a natural leader with no apparent weaknesses. He'd needed to be all that and more to have survived both Judson Drake and Territory Pen and emerge from the crucible looking even more formidable than ever.

Leading the way into the central block, the silent crowds continued to focus on Kelso, who no longer paid them any attention but rather was focused on what comprised the heart of Hardrock dead ahead, with the air of a general surveying the battleground.

None the less some amongst the watchers seemed comfortable with the slowly unfolding drama; Chief Long Bear and the group gathered around him behind the recessed front windows of the Three Deuces, for instance. The Chief was puffing calmly on a long curved pipe carved with Choctaw symbols of fertility, wisdom and mayhem while his sharp brown eyes missed nothing. He'd always gotten along just fine with Creekers in the old days, as he seemed to do with most other rebels, misfits or rangeland poets. And even if Kelso's boys had taken most of their trade down to the Sundowner back then, this at least had ensured the Deuces didn't get trashed by the bunch the way other places had done.

Not all of the Deuces' guests at this congenial mid-morning session of cold beer and easy conversation showed as relaxed as the Chief. Indeed one group of drinkers taking their first ever look at Kelso and company were keenly aware of the tension in the air on all sides now where lazy Saturday-morning camaraderie had prevailed just minutes earlier.

Luke Pike was impressed enough with what he was seeing to comment: 'Thought you claimed these geezers were more like hellraisers than regular badmen, Chief? They shape up as genuine hard pieces of merchandise to me. What say you, Cass?'

'Can't argue with that,' replied Cassidy, looking refreshed and relaxed in a shirt the hotel maid had laundered for him. He cocked an eyebrow at Long Bear. 'Want to take a second guess about this outfit now?'

'I'm not often wrong but I'm right this time,' smiled the

Chief, delighted by his little wordplay. 'Harmless I called them and harmless they still look to these old eyes.' He paused, then added slyly, 'Harmless to me that is. Didn't I add that?'

Waco half grinned. 'Guess you forgot. Anyways, did anyone expect them to just mosey in this way? The way everyone was talking last night seems 'most everybody was expecting these jailbirds to go directly after Drake.' He nodded in the direction of Kelso, who'd stopped his horse before the jailhouse where the marshal stood in the porch shade, arms folded and pale. 'That pilgrim looks to me like he wants to take on the whole damn town.'

Long Bear sobered now. It amused him to take the tribulations of the white man lightly, but only now was he prepared to concede this was not exactly as they'd expected.

'I fear you may be right, Kentucky man. Before, when the feud between the bunch and Pawnee erupted into open warfare, many citizens rightly or wrongly supported Judson Drake in his bid to induct Kelso's acres into his empire. Kelso was very bitter about this at the time of his capture and trial, labelling it as betrayal by his own class.'

'Was it an honest trial?' enquired Pike, thinking back to their recent hair-raising experience with law and order in Sweetwater, Colorado.

The Chief shrugged. 'Perhaps. Nobody really knows what happened the night the shooting began other than that two of Kelso's men were wounded and a third killed. But I do know Drake was able to muster wide support here amongst citizens beholden to him for one reason or another. Some of these sat on the jury while others actively stirred up feeling against the gang, to their eventual cost.' Another shrug. 'Kelso plainly has not forgotten. I thought he would. But I can see that somewhere over the past five years the iron has entered his soul.'

'Like the thirst has entered my throat,' said an easily bored Waco, turning away. 'You still serving, Chief?' He grinned. 'You are if you're genuine Old West, like you claim. The Old West never goes dry, don't you know. I feel like a whiskey.'

So too did Tell Dalton. But the sheriff would have to wait, for plainly Kelso whom he was meeting for the first time today, was not quite through with him yet;

'I got nothin' against you, tinstar,' he advised. 'You weren't around five years ago and I got no reason to believe you're crooked and mean-scared and town-yellow like the badgetoter what helped railroad me and the boys into Territory. I'm back because I got a right to be and there's things I got to do and things I don't. I was done by the law once and won't be again. But if you don't mess with me I'll leave you be. Do we understand one another?'

There was ambiguity in that declaration coupled with an implied threat, neither of which Tell Dalton was prepared to challenge at that moment. Maybe with a double jolt of the Chief's smooth bourbon under his belt he might feel stronger, but then again liquor might erode what little courage he had left.

'I hear you, Mr Kelso,' he said in a strained voice. Then he found some hint of valor salvaged from his younger years; 'I don't want any trouble in my town.'

Kelso seemed not to hear. He turned his horse away from the law office to find doorways, windows, alleymouths and storefronts lined with people. Hardrock seemed at once both fascinated and frightened by what was unfolding. There was reason for this contradiction of reaction. The Creekers had been a dominant factor

106

during the town's most violent era, with Kelso wearing the unofficial insignia of the little man's champion. That status was later conferred upon Jimmy the Boy, two-gun hero of the poor who had kept the kettle boiling and the lawmen jumping, until Fate dealt with him also. Things had been quiet for over a year since under Judson Drake's harsh dominion, often boringly so. Today it seemed many might almost welcome any kind of diversion simply to break the monotony.

'No trouble, the marshal warns!' Kelso's deep-chested voice carried. 'A little too late for that, I'm thinkin'. Or maybe somebody here has a different way of lookin' back to what happened to us here back in the good old days, huh? If you have I'd surely like to hear it.'

There was a scuffling of boots followed by an enormous silence that now contained a kind of ticking in it, as of a big clock, muffled and distant.

Kelso's face appeared twisted as he kneed his mount for the Deuces. He had not planned this day, this way. Back in Territory in the freezing hell of solitary, or rolling on stone floors under the bulls' pounding billy-clubs, he'd schemed a hundred different ways of settling with Drake, clever ways and bloody ways. This decision to simply reappear openly and boldly as was his right, had been made just that morning and acted upon immediately. He now had the satisfaction of knowing it to be the right one. He'd needed this reaction to reaffirm his feeling of power, without realizing it. And he was powerful here; every face told him so.

He dismounted and an avenue opened before him leading to the Deuces' yellow batwings. Bishop, Longhorn, Nathan, Cleal and Brown followed him inside. Breathlessly Maple Street waited for sounds of trouble to erupt from within, and eventually the sound of someone's laughter drifting from the window seemed jarringly anti-climactic.

The biggest street crowd Hardrock had seen since last election eve began to break up after that. Serene and genial at his command post behind the long bar, mine host the Chief predicted record takings from curious citizens who would find themselves unable to stay away from the Deuces now. As was mostly the case, he was proven right.

The partners had been warmed by the way the Chief had accepted them so readily from their first day, almost as though they'd known him all their lives. Yet they were surprised when Kelso seemed to react to them in much the same way following Long Bear's introduction to the man of the moment at the mahogany bar. Kel Kelso was cordial and almost genial towards all three of them, while at the same time continuing to treat most other customers with cold-eyed contempt. Waco, who liked to regard himself as the savvy one, wasn't long in coming up with a theory on why this should be so.

'This guy is either black or white,' he murmured to Cassidy as Kelso and the Chief reminisced in the background. 'If you're pro Drake or ever was then you're all black with this geezer. But if you're agin' Mr Big you're white as the driven snow. We rubbed Pawnee's nose in it over the Turtle so he thinks we're just fine and dandy. Simple.'

'Maybe.'

'For certain. On top of this, there's also the fact that we're newcome here. We ain't tainted with the past, when it seems Drake strong-armed a lot of these towners into sidin' with him against Kelso's mob.' He spread his hands and flashed a grin. 'So he likes us and maybe won't shoot us. Ain't that grand?'

'Whatever you say, man.' Cassidy wasn't paying much attention. Maybe he saw deeper than Waco in this, for he remained unimpressed with Kelso's seeming friendliness, didn't even half-way trust the man. He suspected prison might have pushed a borderline man over the edge. He was aware of the air of menace surrounding the bunch, counterpointed by the patently forced ease of the Deuces' clientele as they sipped their shots, watched and whispered. He also noticed that the crowd now at last appeared to be thinning out for some reason.

He lit another durham, weaved a hand back through his thick hair and wandered out front, where life pulsed slowly through Hardrock in the afternoon. Leaning the point of his shoulder against a porch support, he watched a wide toad of a man with a scrunched-up sunburnt face bring a coach and four in by the Deuces and brake to a halt at the depot. There was a lull before a batch of cowboys from one of the big outfits rode in; he watched a deputy toting a bottle-shaped brown-paper bag across to the jailhouse.

Not many out here on the streets for this time of day either. Big change from when Kelso arrived.

He strolled along Maple to the Diamond Street corner and was considering overlooking the bill of fare at the Greasy Spoon, when he glimpsed a rig emerge from in back of the bank three doors down.

It was a fancy four-wheeled buggy with rubber tyres and brass-rimmed wheels which spun with a flourish as the vehicle cut sharply across the street for an alley-mouth opposite. A four-seater, it was fully loaded, and he identified the banker, the newspaper editor and two well dressed citizens in hard-hitter hats who looked like merchants.

The buggy disappeared and he was left with an impression of almost furtive haste as he turned to retrace his steps back to the central block. He was diverted briefly by a pair of pretty town girls passing by. They smiled at him cheekily then hurried on, giggled at their own boldness.

He looked back over his shoulder, halted. The banker's rig was now visible out on the road which cut by the tannery before veering south by sou'west. This was the road to Pawnee Ranch and the four-wheeler was bowling along at a brisk clip throwing a yellow dust-haze into the sky. A mile beyond the banker's buggy, he could barely make out a brougham drawn by a glossy bay, also heading out.

Cassidy nodded as a thought hit. He stared back along Maple towards the central block. At last maybe he understood why everything seemed so quiet. There simply weren't as many citizens left in town. He had to wonder how many had decided to take a spin out towards the Pawnee on this significant Saturday afternoon, and whether he should read anything sinister into this.

After a moment he shook his head and backtracked to the Greasy Spoon. He was enjoying this eventful day yet still felt the smart thing to do was to put himself outside a platter of sourdough flapjacks, round up the others and head home. Raccoon River instincts warned that Hardrock was not the right place to be today.

It was fitting that the meeting should be held in what was known at Pawnee headquarters as the War Room. A combination of paintings, military memorabilia, the crossed swords and the glowing tapestries depicting Valley Forge and Gettysburg turned the mind towards things martial where problems could be resolved by conflict, heroism and even sacrifice.

The head-count of cattlemen, businessmen and town officials such as marshal and town mayor tallied at around forty by the time Judson Drake strode in and immediately let them know why they had been summoned. Not invited, summoned.

From the outset the big man's manner was overbearing and almost harsh as he summarized the situation in Hardrock. There wasn't a man present not dependent in one way or another upon Drake's patronage, whether this be political, financial or influential. Things had simply evolved that way in Buffalo County. In his climb to the top Drake had taken others with him. Success was his motivation, and though he granted success to others, there was a tab.

Those tabs had first been called in five years ago when Kelso defied Pawnee's attempts to take over Blind Fool Creek Ranch, required by Drake for expansion purposes. When violent conflict resulted Judson Drake was in a position to command allegiance from men from all walks of life including the law and even the judiciary to eventually carry the day against the Creekers and see them hauled away in irons.

How fast could five years go.

It was pure coincidence that saw Kelso's return coincide with the closing stages of the biggest commercial deal the rancher had ever cut. He wished he might overlook the threat; wished fervently he could convince himself that Kelso was just an angry man with a gun while Drake was king of the county.

He could not.

Drake knew men. He was a skilled and ruthless manipulator who knew how to ferret out a man's weaknesses and utilize them for his own benefit. He was successful by nature, and yet this one poorly educated small rancher had proven one of the two most formidable adversaries he'd ever had to deal with. At Kelso's discharge from Territory the warden had described the now ex-king of the cons as 'a dangerous individual of iron will' with an 'almost frightening obsession with all those responsible for his incarceration'.

The other enemy, a baby-faced boy who had once seriously undermined his influence and authority and almost destroyed his own family, was James Justin Kaine. Fortunately Jimmy the Boy was long gone, as he dearly wished Kelso were also. But wishing didn't boil beans. Kelso was in Hardrock this very afternoon with a gun and a gang, apparently whipping up support and sympathy. The great man could feel the wall against his back but, as always under such circumstances, had taken swift and decisive action to deal with a perceived threat; had ordered every man jack present to come to Pawnee and not one had dared refuse. They might well be fearful of the Creekers, but Judson Drake owned them body and soul.

'I am not prepared to wait,' he stated bluntly now, 'until some dark night when a low killer might slip through my security, shinny up a drainpipe and cut my throat ear to ear simply because the law is obliged to wait until someone commits a crime before it can intervene. Would you expect me to do so, sir?'

The marshal flinched in his plush velvet chair when he realized that both the rock-steady finger and the question were aimed directly at him. Dalton had been amongst the very last to respond to Drake's imperious summons to attend his battle briefing, today. Half-drunk and racked with self-loathing, he shook his head. The man Brown had kicked in the window of Cronlow's Store just before Dalton quit town, while he'd actually heard Kelso boasting to the Deuces crowd that he was drinking a brew called 'rich bastard's blood'.

'I reckon I would not, Mr Drake.' The badgeman was ready to stifle his conscience and go along with Drake because he was too weak not to.

But to his surprise and Drake's initial shock, a solid one-third of this hand-picked assembly showed they were not weak. Five years is a long time. They'd supported Drake back then because they were poor and disunited. Now they were strong. Kelso scared the hell out of them, and their spokesman the undertaker made it all too clear that, though loyal, there was no way they were intending to buckle on guns or form something the rancher called a 'people's posse' to take the Creek bunch head on.

'We're sorry, Mr Drake,' he regretted, red-veined eyes refusing to meet the rancher's imperious glare. 'But we ain't gunmen, militiamen or deputies, no sir. We're just law abidin' citizens and you can't expect us to be somethin' we ain't. It jest ain't fair.'

Drake raged. He stormed up and down and made threats he couldn't possibly carry out. He was intimidating, and was made doubly so by the cold eyed presence of Ash Pride and several of the new gunpackers he'd imported to counter the Kelso threat. Yet the hold-outs stood fast. They were united and defiant . . . and underneath all his bluff and bluster Judson Drake felt the actual cold bite of fear.

There was something about men like Kelso and Jimmy Kaine, some kind of charismatic aura surrounding them, that made this man agonizingly aware of his own shortcomings, his vulnerability and his innate cowardice.

Here he was, standing on the brink of elevating himself into the ranks of the ultra-rich and the most powerful in the Territory, yet fearful that it could all be plucked away from him by a revenger's bullet.

But a good gambler never sits down to play without his ace in the hole.

Drake had never anticipated having to use his hole card until now. But with the dusk coming down and the banker's faction refusing to concede, he finally realized there was no choice.

'Very well,' he stated after a long silence in which he managed to achieve some degree of self-control. 'As you will. Much as I detest the disloyal and the avaricious, I will on this occasion make a concession to secure the loyalty I thought every man in this room owed me.'

He paused for effect. The silence was broken by the long-nosed banker whom Drake had elevated from teller to president. This man was deeply indebted to his employer, yet sensed a rare advantage here today.

'I suggest strongly that you make it a serious concession, Mr Drake,' he insisted, revealing to all that monetary gain was at the bottom of his 'moral objections' as it is with all good bankers.

Drake bit into his underlip and appeared haggard yet resigned as he turned his back to haul down a vast colored wall-map of the Hardrock region. He rarely made concessions either in business or his private life, but this was different. Bitterly, petulantly, he recognized a tide running against him that must be stemmed. Now. They heard his sigh as he picked up the cane pointer necessary to indicate certain salient features on his map, then faced them again.

'I guarantee every man in this room five thousand

dollars cash if he agrees to help rid me of these jailhouse scum!'

The War Room went wild.

9
The .45 Solution

The street was theirs. Leastways that was how it felt as Cassidy, Pike and Waco made their light-footed way along the creaking plankwalk, high-heeled boots rapping the boards with a brisk tattoo that was picked up by a big old black man seated on the long front porch of the Frontier with an upturned biscuit tin clasped between his knees. He rapped the tin with smooth-skinned hands and flashed them a white grin as they stomped their heels in time to the beat, and Waco called back, 'Right, old-timer . . . don't let 'em worry you none. Every little thing's going to be just fine. Right?'

'Right, son,' came the response, and Waco punched Cassidy's shoulder and laughed. 'See, what'd I tell you, compañero. It's all blowin' over already. Old Pops there knows it, we know it, and if you take a look round now you'll see 'most everyone does.'

Cassidy was looking. And it seemed to be so. In the early evening-time as the lamplighter made his rounds and the saloons began to hum with music and laughter, Hardrock was plainly returning to something approaching normal at the end of a testing day.

There'd been incidents, sure. A few fights involving the Creekers, some property damage here and there and any amount of unexplained comings and goings out along the Pawnee Ranch trail. But no gunplay or confrontations thus far and now the whole town seemed a little easier even if not totally relaxed as yet.

They passed knots of men smoking and talking quietly on street corners and lounging in the shadowy mouths of the arcades. Faces turned their way as they went by and they were often greeted by name. They were aware that many thought highly of them for besting Judson Drake on the Turtle Ranch purchase . . . as did Kelso. They'd had plenty of well-meaning warnings that the big man would not likely let the matter rest at that, however, although these didn't seem to hold much significance in light of today's developments.

Four men sharing a bench in front of the funeral parlor were deep in conversation and they heard one remark; 'Wonder what Jimmy the Boy would make of this here Kelso situation iffen he was still around. . . ?'

Cassidy glanced back. That name again. Seemed to him that the name of their 'good pal' Jimmy Kaine, even though he was a fugitive on the run, still ran like a stream through everyday life here in the county.

They were picking up their pace as they swaggered by the Hogfoot Café, the bars of light slashing through the louvred doors casting black-and-yellow tiger-stripes across their lithe shapes. Even Cassidy could feel the welcome change in the town's tempo now, and he'd been the one recommending they haul their freight back to Mantrap Valley earlier when the tension was at its peak.

'But are you sure this isn't just the lull before the storm, Abey?' the inner voice of caution whispered. 'Not a chance, it's all settled now,' he muttered aloud, and quickened his stride to keep up with the others.

The decision to chance their luck down at the gambling-hall had been unanimous. Things had gotten a little dull there at the Deuces after the Kelso bunch left for their old stamping-ground of the Sundowner on The Line, so they were primed for some action now. They might well be hardworking men of the land these days, respectable ranchers. But all three were still well short of their twenty-third birthdays, the night was young and the air was filled with music and the scent of sweet grasses giving up their evening odors, mingling with the heady whiff of perfume which grew noticeably stronger and more seductive as they approached the pink-painted building with a red light glowing warmly above the door.

'Ohh, it's them again!' trilled a voice from the shadows. 'Say ain't you-all a-stoppin' by . . . Waco, honey?'

Waco swept off his hat and bowed low from the waist but kept right on walking despite the soft low whistle from a blonde wrapped in a silk kimono on the balcony above.

'How come they know your name?' Pike wanted to know. 'Where'd you get to this afternoon while I was seeing to the horses and Cass was mooning over Arlena Browneyes?'

'Hey look!' Waco diverted them, pointing across the street. 'Looks like that Brown geezer's had enough for one day.'

The blocky figure propped up against a porch support was plainly Mr Brown who was even more plainly drunk as he muttered and swore at passers-by. It occurred to Cassidy that the last time he'd sighted them, none of the other

Creekers showed any signs of over-indulgence. That might seem curious had he taken time to think on it, but who wanted to think on a night like this.

Waco and Pike were joshing one another the way they did when spirits were high . . . and he heard again the voices of old friends and old companions and brothers running the ridges, 'coon hunting along the river in summers that never ended and drowsy afternoon back-stoops where kids played banjos while their older brothers worked at the sawmill. . . .

'For your information, joker,' he grinned at Pike when he could get a word in, as they parted the welcoming batwings to stride in beneath the bright lights of the gambling-hall, 'I wasn't mooning over anybody.'

'Well, you were sure thinking of her, boy.'

He wouldn't deny it. Didn't want to. Arlena Drake was undoubtedly a million miles beyond his reach. But a man could dream. Just a couple of years ago he'd dreamed every night of the Black Hills of Dakota, of riding as a meat-hunter for a wagon train on the Oregon trail, and using his daddy's old 'coon-skinning knife to hack his initials deep into the trunk of a mighty sequoia overlooking a cliff where the Pacific broke against the stones of its ultimate California shore. Well, he'd done all these things and today thought only of an unattainable girl. They were giving up a lot to fit into their new way of life but nobody could stop a man dreaming.

Sweat coursed down Ellis Cleal's straining face as he reached for the crossbar of the telegraph pole. His fingers found purchase and he hauled himself up vigorously to hook one denim-clad leg over the beam. He paused momentarily to catch his breath then hauled the wire-cutters from inside his jacket.

Buck Bishop stood between their horses twenty feet below. He was facing northward where the poles marched off into infinity in the direction of the Big T and Merion. In the opposite direction the lights of Hardrock glowed warmly in the night on the southern horizon.

Cleal snipped twice and there was a soft hissing noise as the severed wires fell into the grass. This was followed by a faint crackling sound from the wires still attached to the crossbar, then silence.

The athlete of the bunch slid down swiftly and Bishop handed him a freshly rolled cigarette.

'Nice work,' he grunted. 'We'd best be gettin' back.'

Cleal's hands shook a little as he cupped the smoke and lighted it. He stared at the other over the flame. 'You think it'll be tonight?'

'Kelso reckons Drake will come after us sooner or later, so we'll be gettin' in sooner.'

'Suits me. I ain't never goin' to rest easy while I've got five years' hard and a dead pard to square accounts for.'

'Makes two of us.'

Moonrise.

From the limitless reaches of the western prairie, silent and swift came the dapple-gray mustang with its black broomtail streaming. The rider in the saddle was young and blue-eyed with an easy way of talking that made folks take to him and his smile opened doors from the Canadian border to the Rio Grande.

Flowing effortlessly across the open grazelands man and horse seemed part of the night itself as they put the swift miles behind them. But as the lights of Hardrock rose

120

up out of the sea of grass ahead the horseman's easy smile seemed to fade and the mustang pricked its ears and slowed as though it too sensed the change.

From a distance Hardrock looked the same as always, a solid and stolid cowtown that would always be a cowtown and nothing else. Yet it was different tonight and the young rider knew it. For he had grown up right here in the county and knew and loved every corner of it in all its moods, prosperous and poor, happy and sad, peaceful and violent.

The horse wanted to run on but a slim hand jerked on the reins to bring it to a sliding halt by the overgrown track leading up to Oakey Hill. Fingering back his hat he hooked one leg lazily over the pommel and just sat gazing across at the town as though settling in for the night.

'Where in damnation is my daughter?'

'We don't know, Mr Drake.'

'Then find out. Pride, that's your job.'

'You know best, Mr Drake. But are you sure you can do without me right now? Tonight?'

The rancher and five gunmen stood in the deep bay-window on the second floor of the Buffalo Cattlemen's Club overlooking Maple Street. The sprawling leather-and-mahogany room lay totally in darkness behind them. From this vantage point it was possible to look over the entire central block from the Greasy Spoon to the Emporium. The Pawnee party and their press-ganged supporters had commandeered the entire club-building two hours earlier, Drake having nominated the plush club as his command post from which he would oversee operations should trouble erupt.

The cattle baron glanced left and right. Dim streetlight

glinted dully off gun-handles, shell-belts, brass cartridge-rims and the lethal sleekness of a blued carbine barrel. He was surrounded by a ring of steel.

'Mr Drake, do you want me to go looking for Arlena or—'

'Stay put, damn you, Pride!' He might be a concerned father but he was not a fool.

Beyond the squat bulk of the tannery to the south where Kelly Street bisected The Line, sprawled an untidy straggle of squalid shacks and dark alleys where Hardrock's losers dwelt. Cotton's Bar was crowded as it was most nights and the mood was turning ugly. Down here on the seamy side of town they were little concerned with happenings uptown with its fine eateries and plush watering-holes such as the Three Deuces. Naturally they were aware that Kelso was back in town, and there was speculation about the risk of a showdown between Pawnee and the Creekers. But whether that long-running feud should erupt again or just fizzle away was of no concern to these. On good old Kelly Street, problems were more immediate and basic. Would Cotton extend a man's tab; who was your woman with tonight; was the blocky stranger at the bar really serious about his challenge to gunfight any man in the place?

Brown was serious; deadly and drunkenly so. Two blocks west along The Line at the Sundowner Saloon at this moment, his former pen-pards from Territory were treating drinks to old pals and admirers and whipping up feeling against Pawnee, exactly as Kelso had so long planned in prison.

Brown was not included.

Kelso claimed he was too drunk, not really up to what the night could bring. They'd let him precede them here to check out the lie of the land and feed that information back to Kelso prior to the bunch's return, but when it came down to cases, they'd just used him. He wasn't good enough to stand shoulder to shoulder with the 'heroes' of Blind Fool Creek.

He would show them. He would show this whole stinking town what he was made of.

He drew his rusty .44 and fired a bullet into the rafters, bringing down a spray of debris and an entire colony of bug-eyed spiders.

'C'mon, it's time this dump showed a bit of life, b'God!' he roared truculently, brandy and bravado making him ten feet tall. 'So on your feet and show this Territory boy just how high you can dance, heh? Unless there's just one *hombre* in this rathole with guts enough to say he won't dance. You in the yeller hat mebbe?'

The smoking gun stormed again and a bottle on a crowded table exploded, spraying men and women with flying fragments, among them Cotton's current love who screamed when she touched her cheek and her hand came away bloody.

The roaring charge from Cotton's sawn-off shotgun took Brown in the shoulder and hurled him to the floor with crimson pumping through his fingers. The man in the yellow hat got to him first and swung a kick to the face that crunched bone. Somehow the dazed Brown squeezed off another shot and a fat man tumbled, clutching a shattered shin bone.

Hardrock's night of terror had begun.

Cassidy had been idly watching the Chief remove bottles from his shelves and place them away beneath the bar for some time before what he was seeing sank in.

'What's the idea, Chief?' he asked over his whiskey glass.

'The idea, young Cassidy, is to protect my stock.'

His next query was automatic. 'From what?' They'd just returned from the gambling hall and were feeling nicely relaxed.

The Indian looked at him curiously. 'Why, from the holocaust, of course. From the fire, the famine, or whatever tribulation descends . . .'

'No, seriously. Why would a saloonkeeper start stashing his supplies away early on a Saturday night?'

The Chief turned sober now. 'You mean you don't know what's going on? You don't know this town is fixing to pop?'

'Pop?' Cassidy swivelled round on his barstool to study the crowd. He felt his neck-hair lift when he belatedly realized that things weren't the same as they'd been earlier, when he'd thought to have a good time. Too many drinkers were watching the doors too steadily now. The Chief had stationed staffers with rifles by the windows and up on the landing. Sure, the Deuces still hummed, but there was something off key in the chink of glassware, the murmur of voices, even the song the little blonde was rendering up on the tiny stage. He swung back sharply. 'What's happening?'

'Kelso's at the Sundowner whipping up his troops against Drake, reminding them of all his past misdeeds. I hear Drake has mustered his forces somewhere here in town in anticipation of the showdown I expect he knows will come.' The Chief shrugged as he took down three green bottles of Old Kentucky bourbon. 'It's all blown up in the past hour since that Brown fellow got shot up at Cotton's Bar.' He winked soberly. 'Take a tip, young

Cassidy, you boys get out of town. Hardrock's troubles
aren't yours.'

He was right, Cassidy tried to convince himself as he
made his way back out on to the lamplit street. They'd
been here but a month, so whatever was brewing didn't
concern them.

He halted on the porch where a big man in a yellow
poncho lurched past looking anxiously over his shoulder.

Now he'd been alerted to the situation, Cassidy was
sharply attuned to every nuance of change that had overtaken the main street just in an hour or two. It was in the
air, in the faces of the men at the windows. A shoot-up on
Kelly Street, the Citizens' Club bulked in darkness, a haze
of smoke now hanging over the area below The Line.
They'd simply been having too damn good a time to
notice. But of course none of it had anything remotely to
do with them.

He nodded his head to emphasize this point, yet knew
he wasn't fooling anyone but himself. Hardrock and
Buffalo County was their new home, forget how long or
short a time they'd been here. They'd made it theirs and
had been accepted, surprisingly warmly by many. A man
didn't adopt a place then turn his back at the first whiff of
trouble.

Arlena!

The thought hit with the speed of a thrown knife. He
stiffened, glancing back through the windows at the
Chief's totemic figure calmly drawing beer behind the bar.
Long Bear believed the showdown between Kelso and
Drake was imminent. If so, how could that not pose a
threat to Arlena?

He'd entered the Deuces just minutes earlier in care-
free mood with a five-dollar blackjack win in his pockets,

was now a grimly sober man with urgency in his step as he cut across the street for the Cattleman's.

Abe Cassidy needed to know just what was brewing in his town.

The two-storied clubhouse was bolted up tight, its darkness unnatural, even ominous. The fact that he found nothing there failed to reassure him any, and his mouth was dry as he hurried on, driven by a sense of urgency he didn't quite understand.

The jailhouse door stood wide open yet he found no reassurance there. The contrary rather. What he did find was a party of agitated citizens urging the marshal to take action to head off the dangerous situation they also feared was building up to a climax. To no avail. Tell Dalton was working on another agenda named John Barleycorn.

'My hands are tied, gentlemen,' he slurred, unaware of Cassidy framed in the doorway. 'A man went on a shooting spree on The Line and paid the price. That is my official finding. Apart from that there have been no further incidents warranting my attention . . .'

'You're in Drake's pocket!' a red faced merchant accused. 'We're tellin' you Drake's forted up at the club with half his crew and every citizen he can muster. They are primed ready to take on that mob Kelso's whippin' up down at the Sundowner . . . and you say your hands are tied? Where's your sense of duty, Marshal?'

'What can one man do?' Dalton said wretchedly. He lurched to his feet at the muffled report of a shot. 'Where did that come from. . . ?' He stared from face to face then suddenly brightened. 'You are right, you know, gents. Most likely it is getting out of hand.' He reached for his hat on the rack, almost falling in the process. 'An emergency, in other words, and in an emergency I'm entitled to summon assistance from Merion. Out of my way, boys, I'm going to wire the Commissioner's Militia.'

'Goddamnit, Dalton, you must be drunker than you look even,' the blacksmith almost snarled. 'The telegraph's been out the past hour. They reckon the wires must be down. We're cut off here with Kelso and Drake squarin' off and our peace officer drunker'n a brewer's cat . . .'

Urgency gripped Cassidy hard as he swung away to pause momentarily by the hitch rail. Pike and Waco were still at the roulette wheel, riding a streak. The hall lay a block beyond the Sundowner along The Line.

He darted nimbly between two horsemen travelling south along Maple and jogged the remainder of the way to the Sundowner.

He didn't go in, lunging to a halt beneath the saddler's awning directly opposite.

The mob spilling out onto the saloon porch was made up of cowboys, day-laborers, timber-cutters, hunters, miners and just plain salooners. Kelso people. Five years earlier the hardcases of Blind Fool Creek comprised the rebel weft in the fabric of Buffalo County. They were tough and independent, lone riders who often bucked both Pawnee and the law and got away with it. When they'd gone to prison the everyday working man had been left without focus or leadership until Jimmy the Boy came to the fore, his courage and championing of the little man elevating him higher even than Kelso had ever stood. Since Kaine's death Pawnee Ranch had stood unchallenged for a year and more. Until tonight.

But this bunch wasn't simply excited to have Kelso back amongst them and boosting their spirits; Cassidy saw that plainly. They were primed, angry and ready for action, and he was given an inkling howcome when Kelso emerged with Bishop, Longhorn, Nathan and Cleal in back of him. The Blind Fool Creek boys were pumping their fists and chanting; 'Drake's gotta go! Drake's gotta go!'

A bearded tannery-hand bellowed back, 'He's been gyppin' us and bleedin' us white through his lousy bank and stealin' our land and—'

'And sending innocent men to jail!' Kelso roared in a voice laced with hate.

'How many good men's he sent to the poorhouse?' howled another.

'And that black dog murdered Jimmy Kaine, by God and by Jesus he did! And the boy's death ain't never been avenged 'til this day!'

Whoever yelled this last touched a nerve. The watching Cassidy saw Kelso's face light up triumphantly when the crowd reacted as though touched by a communal goad. Although well fired-up before, suddenly it seemed some germ of hidden violence in the night was uncovered and erupted into healthy, shambling life. It showed in the eager sweaty face of a man who leapt up on to a wagon firing his gun into the sky. It was there in the excited faces of the painted women shrieking encouragement from the saloon porch. Before his eyes he saw some two-score people transformed into a single entity. He was staring at the face of the mob, one of the ugliest sights on earth.

By the time Kelso shouldered his way through and strode along the rutted street heading for Maple, taking his rag-tag-and-bobtail army of underdogs with him, the saddler's porch was empty.

Pike and Waco were still at the wheel, too dazzled by their success against the odds to pay much attention to wars or rumors of wars. Until a white-faced Cassidy yanked them outside and led the way for Main Street, that was.

Cassidy talked fast.

It was not just one sober head that reached the central block several minutes later, but three. Although Cassidy had warned them what to expect, Waco and Pike still blinked disbelievingly when they first sighted the mob now drawn up a block west to be harangued by the familiar figure of Kelso standing upon a flatbed wagon. Citizens were fleeing along the walks and a woman screamed somewhere. They could now make out dim shapes with rifles atop the flat roof of the Cattlemen's Club building across from the Deuces.

'Jumped up Judas!' Waco breathed. 'What are we goin' to do?' As though he too felt somehow personally responsible for their new hometown. He swung sharply on Cassidy. 'Side with Drake . . . if he's forted up at the club? We can't stand by and let a pack of wild dogs take over, man.'

'Got no choice,' insisted a grim-faced Luke Pike. He hauled his shooter. 'Well, leastways our pard the drifter showed us more about lookin' out for ourselves than we ever—'

'Put that damn thing away!' Cassidy said angrily, chopping down on Pike's forearm. 'Didn't we learn anything at Sweetwater? We had trouble there and tried to settle it our way, and came within a whisker of stretching rope . . .'

He paused as three men rushed by. They wore weapons but didn't have them in hand. They were running scared. Hardrock was lurching wildly out of control before their eyes, something ugly and undeniable rising out of the rough boards and streets. He'd felt it at the Sundowner; it was even stronger here on Maple.

'Well, what do we do if we don't fight?' Waco challenged. 'No law, no telegraph, now we're not supposed to shoot anybody. Where to from here, *amigo?*'

Quite suddenly and with crystal clarity, Cassidy knew he had the answer.

It was almost exciting to be galloping through unknown country in the middle of the night as they'd used to do so often for the simple thrill of it. Ignoring the Keep Out signs posted at intervals along the southern border-fence of the off-limits Big T Ranch, they'd busted through a gate on to the spread miles back; now they employed all their trail skills to select the best route to navigate scrub, brush, arroyo, gully and draw, occasionally startling the odd bunch of cattle.

Nobody ever attempted the Big T shortcut these days, they'd been warned back at the livery. Free access had been available once, but the rough-country spread had been off limits for almost six months now. Nobody seemed to know why.

The partners were putting it back in limits, calculating that by following the telegraph line which naturally followed the shortest route across the big spread, they would trim off an hour to an hour and a half riding-time to reach the garrison of the Commissioner's Militia at Merion and get them headed back for Hardrock.

Clem Waco rode forward scout with .45 in hand. The liveryman had warned that trespassers had been shot at up here. They couldn't understand why. Waco had seen better dirt under his fingernails. But one thing was for sure, and Abe supported him on this; no trigger-happy hick cowboys were going to stop them tonight. Not with their new hometown depending on them getting through fast, they weren't.

A string of swift miles had been put behind them before they glimpsed a strange glow through a fork in the hills dead ahead. They slowed, frowning in puzzlement. Big T headquarters was supposed to be miles further on and well off to the north-west. They'd anticipated nothing but dreary cow-country and raddled low hills most of the way to the ranch's northern boundary, just south of Merion.

The glow grew stronger as they pushed on, dropping from gallop to lope to trot and finally back to a shuffling walk mere moments before they heard something that brought them jerk-reining to a dead halt beneath the spreading branches of a peppercorn tree.

Quite clearly and distinctly what they heard was the unmistakable sounds of a slow-moving train!

Side by side they bellied through coarse knee-high grass hard by the right of way. The shock of finding themselves in the center of a railroad construction-site with dim valley walls flanking low on either side and the telegraph posts marching directly by alongside the twin ribbons of steel reaching as far northward as could be seen by night, was beginning to wear off by now. They had to accept it as crazy and impossible, then take it from there, Cassidy supposed.

How could you throw up a railroad without anybody knowing about it? Who would try? And why?

They hugged mother earth and froze at the sound of boots crunching the uneven slag boulders of the roadbed. Not seeming to breathe, they rolled their eyes upwards to watch a big man with a heavy keyring on his belt and a Winchester tucked beneath his arm tramp slowly by. His shadow cast by the pole lights cut across their prone bodies, then was gone.

Waco nudged him in the ribs. 'Security. Maybe that's all they've got this time of night. One geezer standin' watch. Who'd ever come here anyway? Who'd want to?'

Warily Pike lifted his head. 'He went into one of the shacks. Don't see anybody over by the car.'

The car was their objective. For after adjusting to the lamplit spectacle of tie-piles, rock buggies, mule corrals, forges, toolsheds, rows of workmen's shacks and the short stubby black work-locomotive chuffing and clanking along a side-track billowing steam and smoke, they had concentrated their attention on the luxurious Pullman car standing at the loading landing. The attraction of the handsome green car with its burnished gold roof was not its sheer incongruity out here beneath the stars, but rather something sharp-eyed Waco had spotted first, namely twin connecting wires running down from a telegraph pole into what appeared to be the smallest of the car's three compartments.

They couldn't believe their luck.

Time enough to puzzle on the very improbability of the railroad's existence at another time, they'd decided. What signified was that it appeared they had stumbled across a telegraph hookup a good two hours' riding-time south of Merion. Two hours quicker making contact, at least four hours off their estimated travelling time to their destination there and back, if this was so.

Bedstones snagged on their clothing as they belly wriggled on. They were snaking past an area dotted with tents and light wood-and-canvas shacks, workers' accommodation by the looks. At one point Pike tapped Cassidy on the shoulder and jerked his chin in the direction of a strip of fencing in back of the tents. It stood around six feet high with barbed wire strung along the top. But further out beyond the cleared area could be seen a squat log-and-daub construction with rifle slits in the walls resembling a bunker of some kind.

They traded looks. A man could be forgiven for mistaking this track-end for a closely guarded prison work-gang.

Finally the car loomed above them. They waited to catch their breath, listening, eyes darting every which way. Nothing was to be heard but the self-important loco now doing mysterious nocturnal things in a big tin shed that seemed to magnify its asthmatic wheezing. It suddenly emerged, drawing a short line of boxcars, flatcars and gondolas, swung round a loop and click-clacked away.

They looked up.

Light showed through the window shades of what they hoped would prove to be a communication point. There were steps leading up to each of the three compartments, one of which had silk curtains at the windows slightly parted showing a crystal bowl filled with wildflowers. Someone here liked their fixings prime.

Cassidy grunted and they began clambering up the third set of steps, then halted abruptly. Directly above the partly open door, between the window-line and the curved roof-edge of the car, was a brass plaque which read; BUFFALO-WESTERN RAILROAD.

They eased inside. The plush fittings confirmed their first impressions of style and luxury. The car's three compartments were separated by sliding doors. Two doors were closed but the one they were interested in stood partly open.

Waco led the way in and pressed his gunsights hard

against the temple of the clerk dozing on a bunk alongside his telegraph key.

Pike closed the door behind them as the man jerked awake. 'Take it easy, joker,' Cassidy whispered. 'We're friendlies and this is an emergency. So get your key working.'

'Y-yessir.' The man was so scared he was biting his tongue. He filled his chair and clicked his key. 'Where to?'

'Merion.'

It went without a hitch. The telegrapher was too frightened to do anything but follow instructions, and they were ready to leave mere minutes later after receiving the receipt-of-message signal from the Merion telegraph office. But Waco hesitated. He motioned to Luke to keep watch through a small window, nodded down at the man in the chair.

'I saw a sign outside, pilgrim. Who's building this track?'

'Why, Buffalo Investments and Western Rail, sir.'

'Who's Buffalo Investments?'

'Mr Drake from Hardrock.'

'Come on,' Cassidy hissed urgently, sliding open the door. 'Someone coming.'

This time there were two security men. They had reached the car and stood below the door muttering and looking about. Plainly they'd seen or heard something; maybe the horses. Peering down through the little round window in the door, Cassidy stiffened as the taller of the pair hooked a meaty hand onto a grab rail and started up the steps.

They allowed him to open the door and Luke Pike swiped him hard with his gun-butt. The man fell with a crash and the telegrapher emitted a squawk of alarm.

Waco reefed the door open as the second man looked up with a startled shout. Waco hurled himself down upon him and they went rolling off the roadbed in a tangle of arms and legs, raising what to a fast-alighting Cassidy and Pike sounded loud enough racket to wake the county.

The guard was big and husky and it took several solid hits to put him away, by which time the track-end of the Buffalo and Western Railroad Company was jolting into life: whistles screeching and dogs barking furiously. But half-awake gradelayers proved no match for three quick-silver Kentuckians who were always at their best acting out the fantasy roles they'd created for themselves so often back along Raccoon River.

Even so, bullets were whistling dangerously close through the scrubby trees by the time they reached the draw where the horses were tied. They didn't return fire, simply filled leather and raked with spur. The loco's whis-tle attached to the side of its huge pear-shaped stack emit-ted a furious scream which frightened the horses and had them breaking into full gallop through the type of shad-owy and rough terrain where normally even a canter would be too fast for safety.

But roan, chestnut and dun kept their footing and the riders somehow stayed in the saddle. They were still not out of the woods as they went storming across a grassy swale, yet when Waco turned his head and flashed a big grin his partners smiled back. They had not travelled all that far from Tennessee, still believed if it wasn't fun the game just wasn't worth the candle.

Hardrock lay twenty-five miles away.

On a level stretch they stopped to blow the horses. It was colder, coming on towards first light, and there wasn't a star to be seen in the whole steel arch of the sky. As soon as the horses were easy again, they pushed on. Cassidy felt his crumple-eared chestnut's shoulders pumping as they dipped into a long and narrow draw. When they emerged, the air smelt of smoke.

10

Who Sleeps on Oakey Hill?

In the half-light of the doctor's front parlor, Kelso looked more than ever like a man composed of something much harder than mere flesh and blood.

'Get up!' he ordered, lips curled back from big strong teeth.

'Kel,' Tommy Longhorn groaned, half rising from the bloodied bench, 'I'm hit bad, man. Ask the doc.'

'He's in no condition for whatever it is you have in mind, Mr Kelso.' Bespectacled, weary and with more injured awaiting his attention, Hardrock's diminutive medico was too disgusted to sound anything but contemptuous. He might have saved his breath. He believed the violence had gotten completely out of hand, but Kelso was just warming to it.

'We're hitting the Cattlemen's again,' he told his shot-up henchman. He raised a finger. 'Listen.'

He wasn't a king, but every man's friend,
'Cept the law and the rich man who brought his sad
    end . . .

Somehow Longhorn managed to heave himself up on one elbow to squint through the window at the street. The mob from the Sundowner were coming down Maple, marching in uneven ranks, and with a semblance of the martial in their workday Levis and wide-brimmed hats. Some were wounded and many were missing, believed cowardly, following the first vicious battle at the fortified club. Several men toted blazing torches which flung their shadows hugely across the façade of the darkened hotel. Most brandished weapons and angry faces gleamed shiny and crimson-hued in the torchlight as they swung on to the inspiring rhythm of 'Young Jimmy Kaine'.

'We've lost half, either hurt or yeller,' Kelso bit out savagely. 'But you, me, Nathan and three miners are takin' the rear while the Sundowners hit the front. So on your feet, Tommy.'

Tommy Longhorn tried to respond but the strength just wasn't there to bring him upright. Kelso's vicious back-hander knocked the man from the bench to the floor. He drew his .45 and for a breathless moment the medic, the injured lining the wall, and his Blind Fool Creek pard of twenty years' standing all believed he would shoot.

Longhorn was likely saved by the sudden racket of gunfire from the street. Kelso spun and was gone, leaving the doctor and his assistant to heave the wounded man back on to the bench. The hardcase was more shocked than hurt.

'Kel's gone over the edge,' he gasped. 'It . . . it nigh happened a couple times in Territory . . . now it's got him by the short hair. It's the hate, y'know. Sure, we all got reason to hate Drake's guts, but Kel's let it eat him out until there's nothin' else . . . and there's nothin' can stop him . . .'

He broke off to cough blood as a splintering crash punctuated the rumble of violence spilling in from the street. The noise was that of the barricaded rear door of the Cattlemen's Club caving in under the third driving blow of an improvised battering ram – a corner post from the fence – wielded by Cleat Nathan, a trio of miners, and Kelso.

The assault team dropped the post and grabbed out their six-guns as murderous gunfire erupted from within. Rifle-lead ploughed into porchboards and uprights, slammed into the screen wall and pulverized the hanging flower-pots that club staffers were cultivating in back.

Nathan sagged with a slug in him someplace and Kelso lunged desperately sideways behind a bucking Colt .45 as hot lead scorched his short ribs and chopped a hole through his bandanna. He struck the ground rolling and kicked away to make it to the safety of the corner as his miners panicked and cut for cover across the alleyway.

Kelso's curses were swallowed by an explosion from somewhere close by. Men from the Sundowner who'd found the siege of the Cattlemen's too lethal for their tastes had settled for torching Drake properties along Maple. The explosion erupted in the warehouse in back of the general store where explosives were stored, and Kelso could feel the billowing heat from the fire as he legged it down a side lane to reach Maple, where he was almost run down by dark figures rushing away from the club.

'Pride just downed Joey and Wilson!' howled a bearded buffalo-hunter, who just hours before had been a belligerent, torch-toting leader in the march. 'They got too much firepower in there—'

His shout was chopped off as Kelso's gunbarrel slashed across his forehead, opening it to the bone. Kelso attempted to kick the man as he fell but was jolted off balance by another runaway following close behind. Snarling, he aimed and jerked trigger. The hammer clicked on an empty, and he was fumbling for shells from his belt when a combination of disappointment and exhaustion hit him harder than a bullet. In the dying hours of the longest day of his life, the iron man from Blind Fool Creek could feel it all draining out of him in a rush; the energy, the power, the sheer will to go on, as his tall figure slumped against a wall and his shaven head tilted back.

He didn't see the turmoil in the street any longer, was heedless of the raging blaze consuming the biggest store in fifty miles with flames leaping a hundred feet into the air. The broken windows, the fires that had begun then died out, the choking smoke and the sporadic crash of gunfire seemed ghostly and muted to his senses and only The Hole was real. . . .

Solitary. It had been down there in that stone ice-hole beneath the penitentiary flagstones that his hatred for one man had become something stronger and all-consuming until it became everything, the very reason to go on living. It moulded him into something stronger and more dangerous than anything the prison had seen before. Yet the cost had been immense. Little by little the finer qualities that had characterized him were honed away to be replaced by the single passionate objective. Survive, get back, destroy the man who'd ruined his life and retrieve all those things Judson Drake had stolen from so many good men, from an entire county. Land, self-respect, freedom.

In the triumphal visions he experienced in the eternal darkness of The Hole his cause had always been crowned by ultimate success, culminating in an almost infantile vision of himself riding down Maple Street at the head of his heroic bunch, accepting the plaudits of a grateful town.

His head came down and he blinked almost painfully.

Maple Street lay before him but there was nobody waiting to place the victor's laurel wreath on his brow. The sounds of conflict had receded and it was growing quieter and darker. The Cattlemen's Club, fortified by Drake and all those he'd coerced into standing by him, still stood, scarred but defiant.

He twitched like a horse touched by a goad. They were losing, perhaps had already lost. And for the first time in many years, maybe since childhood, a single tear coursed down the bronzed cheek of the hardest man in Buffalo County as the possibility of failure, shame, humiliation and possibly death reached him at last.

The unique moment was quickly past. Dashing at his eyes, he straightened and sucked in a huge lungful of acrid smoky air. Standing tall, he returned to his reloading. No fumbling now. He was mechanically quick and efficient, his deliberation almost frightening.

With two full Colts in his hands he turned and strode through the smoke towards the Cattlemen's Club.

They were too late.

That was their first reaction as leg-weary horses slowed to a halt at the junction of Maple and Diamond. On one side were the charred and still smoking remains of what had been the offices of Drake Enterprises, on the other was the brightly lit surgery of the medico with his long front porch crowded with silent men waiting attention for their wounds.

Most everyplace else but at this junction the citizens of Hardrock were locked indoors, peering out fearfully, mourning the town and peaceful way of life that had been theirs. Somewhere a woman wailed like an Apache squaw following a massacre.

Wordlessly Cassidy heeled his horse on and his partners followed, clop-hoofing down the central block. Here and there people were slowly beginning to emerge, some to stare dumbly at the damage, others to stand against the rosy sky with arms outstretched to the heavens in relief or prayer. Others knelt or skulked into alleys as the riders approached. It was eerie to see an entire town in a state of shock.

The Cattlemen's Club and the Three Deuces faced one another across the littered street, the former battered and scarred with every window broken, the latter with the Chief standing on the porch puffing his long-stemmed pipe, virtually untouched.

They reined in, staring. 'I wouldn't be resting up if I were you, young Cassidy,' Long Bear said calmly, as though he'd been standing there just waiting for them to show. He removed his pipe and jabbed the stem southwest. 'Drake retreated to Pawnee around dawn, thinking it was all over. So did I. But Blue Feather here . . .' he indicated the Choctaw handyman standing motionless by the batwings, '. . . he saw someone he believed to be Kelso trailing the party out.'

Cassidy just shrugged. 'So?' He felt a hundred. Felt that everything, the brutal ride, the dangers they'd survived to relay their plea for help – everything had been for nothing. 'What's that to me?'

The Chief met his eyes levelly. 'Miss Arlena was with her father, who is wounded.'

Blended whiskey trickled down Ash Pride's smoke roughened throat. It was the best liquor money could buy yet
tasted like gall. Even so he still poured another, the heavy
bottle clunking as he wearily replaced it on the bar by his
six-gun. His two remaining gunhands slumped on plush
barstools either side of him, staring at the early light filter-
ing through the pure-silk drapes of the War Room.

The gunmen didn't talk.

Their employer was still alive and they'd gotten him
safely back to the ranch, only to find it abandoned by fearful cowboys. Nobody knew if they should be celebrating a
victory or mourning a defeat. It wasn't known how many
others had been killed, wounded or had bolted from town
in funk. The night just past was a blurred montage of the
siege at the Cattlemen's Club, of raging drunks with guns
and torches in the street, of courage and cowardice and
the stink of smoke and blood. Three of the most dangerous guntippers in Buffalo County slumped like old men in
the county's finest room waiting for somebody to return
from town to enable an assessment of the uncertain situation to be made, for the blended bourbon to do its heal-
ing work.

At least they had the satisfaction of knowing Kelso was
dead, or so they wanted to believe. Sometime during the
madness he'd struck the damaged south flank of the club
in a single-handed attack that saw good men scythed down
under his flaming guns, until Pride had cut him down.
The mob's momentum had flagged from that point on
until a seemingly bullet-proof Jimmy Kaine appeared in
Maple Street to rally them yet again, at which point Pride
and Drake decided upon their 'strategic withdrawal' to

Pawnee. It was possible that towards dawn the battle of Hardrock had ended in a whimper rather than a bang.

'Pass the bottle, Ash.'

'Get it yourself.'

No post-battle camaraderie here. These men were pros, linked only by circumstance. Pride had a bullet in his leg and another man nursed a bloody shoulder-wound. They were used up, played out and uncaring, no way for fighting men to be until colors were struck and the outcome posted.

They didn't see where he came from. One moment the three had the big room to themselves, the next they had company of the worst kind.

Kelso seemed to first emerge, ghostlike and insubtstantial, with the pearly light sifting through an eastern window, then he assumed all too human form before them. He was hatless with a bloodied bandanna knotted round his shaven skull, was limping from a second bullet in the thigh, yet somehow managed to appear more invincible than ever as he stared at them over naked guns.

'Go ahead, scum,' he urged softly. 'It's three to one. This could be your lucky day . . . who knows?'

While Pride and the second man froze, the third gun, a square block of a man with a blue jaw, slowly and deliberately began lifting his heavy revolver from the bartop, almost like someone in a trance. Kelso allowed the long-barrelled Walker .44 to rise to within an inch of firing-level, then shot him through the shoulder, dropping him to the floor.

Gray-faced and disbelieving, Ash Pride darted a lightning hand to the gun on the bar as he reared up from his stool. The gun came up faster than seemed possible, yet the gunfighter's surge of hope lasted only a second. Three

144

soft-nosed slugs stitched across his shirtfront and the smoking six-gun swung away from him to empty its last two slugs into the back of the third man streaking for the door.

The room was still reverberating to the thud of the falling body when Kelso heard it. The patter of running steps. Whirling away from the bar and limping round the great Queen Anne table with all its locked secrets, the man from Blind Fool Creek went awkwardly along the polished hallway, punching fresh shells into his Colt. He lunged out through the gaping front doors to see the slim figure of the girl assisting an unsteady man through spilling sunshine towards the handsome four-wheeled buggy which stood, still unharnessed, at the snubbing post outside the stables fifty yards distant.

And Kelso smiled in a way he had not done in five years, was in an instant a whole man free of pain, weakness or human uncertainty, as he went out after them. With dried blood caking one side of his face, his pants leg soaked in crimson and blue-metal Colts back snug in their holsters, he was at once avenger and victor.

The moment was his.

Kelso flexed big hands as Arlena Drake turned to see him. She cried out. He laughed aloud when a grimed and blood-spattered Drake also turned, and he saw a frightened old man shaking in terror who began to whimper like a sick girl.

This was even better than his finest dream. Drake broken first *then* dying at his hands. Immeasurably better than even his sickest imaginings!

He felt so fine he wasn't even limping now as he strode out with the sun in his face, snorting with suppressed laughter, as, in attempting to clamber up, Drake slipped and struck his head hard on the steel buggy-step and slumped to earth before his daughter could support him.

The horseman appeared so swiftly from in back of the big hip-roofed barn concealing the trail that Kelso snatched out his right-hand gun instinctively even before lifting his left to shade his eyes. His murderous scowl quickly faded as he allowed the .45 to slide back into leather.

'And what brings you out here, young Cassidy? Thought you'd hightailed it to Merion or some such fool- ishness.' His tone was amiable. They'd met and mingled easily under the umbrella of the Chief's bonhomie at the Deuces. Cassidy and his pals called themselves cattlemen but they reminded Kelso more of wild boys such as he and the Creekers had been . . . an eternity ago.

Cassidy didn't glance towards the buggy as he slid to ground. He dare not take his gaze from the man before him. The sun was at his shoulder and Kelso looked too tall, too assured and too purely lethal to be real with the sun in his face. He looked supremely invincible in that moment.

Then he shot a quick glance over his shoulder. Someone had been trailing him out the last couple of miles. He mightn't have much time . . .

'Howdy, Kelso.' His voice was remarkably steady for a man likely staring death in the face, his stance seemingly relaxed. Then he held up his left hand, palm forward. 'Guess you better hold up right there.'

'No, Abel!' Arlena cried in terror. 'Please . . .'

'What's the score, kid?' Kelso wasn't smirking now. 'Are you—?' He broke off, cutting a sharp glance in the direc- tion of the buggy. 'Oh yeah, slipped my mind. Didn't I hear tell you and Miss Pretty here were kinda friendly? Sure I did,' he added, something cruel flaring in his eyes now. 'Well, I got nothin' against her or you, kid. Matter of

146

fact, come to think on it, I'm about to do you a big favor. When I'm through with him all this can be yours, includin' her, if you want.'

He started for the buggy again but Cassidy's voice halted him.

'Leave it go, Kelso. You've done enough, man. And I . . . I'm not letting you do any more.'

'You?' Kelso turned disbelievingly. 'You'd try and stop me?' He made a dismissive gesture. 'Go on home, son. You're a kid playin' a man's game. Get back to the hills while you can still—'

'You're not killing this man, Kelso!' His voice was no longer reasoning. He stood with feet apart and his hand near his gun. He licked his lips and added, 'I'll stop you if I have to.'

'You – stop *me*?' Kelso was incredulous. Then his face blanked for a moment to be replaced with a look of total loathing. This was the Kelso of Territory's Black Hole raging at Cassidy from out of his own private hell-hole of agony and hate. 'Well, by God and by Judas, the Chief was sure wrong about you. And to think he likened you to Jimmy the Boy. That's rich! You are just another Drake crawler and that's goin' to cost you. Better take out that gun you're playin' with as I'm a-goin' to kill you – *boy*!'

Abe Cassidy knew he must die even as he went for iron. Despite Jimmy Kaine's patient tutoring, he felt slow and ponderous as his six-gun came clear. But in reality he was youthfully swift and totally desperate enough to execute the draw and fire of a lifetime that saw an over-confident Kelso stagger back a step with dust puffing from his shirt-front. But Kelso's right hand gun was blossoming fire and Cassidy spun and fell with hot agony scorching his ribs. He was hurt and helpless and already his senses seemed to be playing him tricks as he glimpsed what appeared to be a beam of crimson light streak by from somewhere behind him, accompanied by what sure sounded like the awful roar of a sixshooter.

Kelso staggered and his haunted eyes snapped wide with disbelief as Cassidy whirled to see the man he now knew as Jimmy Kaine riding up on his broomtail with a smoking Colt in either hand.

'Jimmy, you Judas!' Kelso's face suppurated with fury. He was down on one knee with blood soaking his shirt-front, but the big revolver in his hand was as steady as the Rock of God. '*This* ain't how it's supposed to end, damn you, boy!'

He triggered and Kaine flinched in his saddle. But this was legend versus legend and Jimmy Kaine had always been king in this county. Tight-lipped and white-faced he calmly fired twice, the shots coming so close together they sounded as one. Kelso's body leapt forward in an awful spasm of final energy, then settled slowly, the dust receiving him gently, never to move again.

At another time, Abe Cassidy would begin to understand why Arlena came rushing across to him, skirts flying, eyes wild with fear and crying his name, while Jimmy Kaine sat his bloody saddle, watching, with one hand pressed against his side.

But that would be later. All that was important at that moment was that somehow he'd survived, that it all might well be over at last ... that her hands were soft as a Kentucky twilight as they cradled his face. And, woman-like, accused him fiercely of the unforgivable sin of 'wanting to play hero'.

He laughed at that, even though it hurt. There was only one hero out here, that was for certain-sure. But when he

148

finally got to sit up and look about, Jimmy Kaine was nowhere to be seen.

They welcomed the rain. It helped erase the burnt stink of Hardrock and seemed to sluice away the leftover legacy of the anger and violence that had polluted their good town.

And it was a good town underneath, always had been. A greedy man and the most dangerous of his many victims may have combined to create a climate of conflict which had reached its fierce climax three nights earlier, but now already the memories were fading. The funerals were all behind them, although the doc was still working daylight to dusk trying to save some of the survivors. But a sober Tell Dalton was back on the streets again and carpenters were hard at work at half a dozen locations along Maple. Chief Long Bear was fishing down at the river beneath a huge umbrella painted by hand to look like appaloosa hide.

The county commissioner continued to work at unravelling the last of the major mysteries at a big cluttered desk in the jailhouse and his uniformed militiamen assisted the dazed citizenry on the streets. The telegraph was operating again, which facilitated the commissioner's task of transmitting and receiving information pertinent to the shedding of light on so many matters which both the law and Hardrock demanded to understand; those deals, schemes, plots and deceptions of Judson Drake's engineering which had already proven to be at the root of every major trouble and injustice experienced here in the recent past.

The so called 'secret railroad', for instance. Maps, contracts and other documents seized under commissioner's privilege from both the railroad and the 'war room' at Pawnee, revealed only too plainly how Drake had formed a covert partnership with Western Railroad to construct a line from Merion to Hardrock in order to turn the latter into the preferred shipping-point for the Texas herds.

The line had to be kept secret both to stop Merion attempting to prevent the construction of the track, which would spell ruin for that town when completed, and also to enable Drake to gobble up every inch of spare real estate in Hardrock, which would rocket in value the day the first cattle train steamed into town.

Western Railroad, Pawnee and Big T Ranch had worked effectively together in this covert partnership and might well have achieved all their goals had not the Creekers been released from Territory when they were. The timing had proven fatal. For now Kelso was dead and Drake was facing many a long day in court over suspect land- and property-dealings, extortion and coercion; was even accused of employing force and threats to make the new owners of Turtle Ranch sell their piece of land. By far the most serious charge he would have to face was that of tampering with the justice system in the celebrated trial of one James Kaine just over a year earlier. His daughter had already volunteered to stand as a witness for the prosecution in this matter.

The county commissioner had summoned the Kentuckians the previous day to brief them on developments, as well as to explain Drake's interest in the Turtle. With the help of a map he illustrated how Drake had planned to induce the Texas herders driving up the Western Trail to veer north-west for Merion a good eighty miles south of their current turning-off point north of the Comanche Hills. The detailed new maps outlined the course of Drake's proposed new cattle trail, beginning at Rosswater and traversing the empty breadth of the Indian Prairie before making the steep short ascent up Clawhammer Pass and across Mantrap Valley. This was the sole navigable route through the Comanches, offering access to the plains and Hardrock.

Without Turtle in his possession Drake's entire plan could have collapsed should the new owners elect not to allow either free or tithed access across their land. And being Judson Drake, he'd had to have it all, not just most of it. It was the only way he knew.

Later, much later, a sober Abe Cassidy sat with Arlena on the chief's jetty watching him cast his line with infinite Choctaw patience. The sun was low and the young woman at his side seemed remarkably composed for someone who had just seen her father off for Territory Penitentiary in a prison-hospital van. Yet Cassidy understood. They'd been rarely out of one another's company over the past days, drawn together by a terror shared and something more. He knew he loved her, only wished he could discuss with her what had happened at the ranch house and hopefully find out just how she felt now about Jimmy Kaine, not seen since the shootout. Deep down he knew he was afraid to do so for what he might learn. For after all, the romance between Jimmy Kaine and Arlena Drake was so much part of life here as to have become enshrined in legend, hadn't it?'

'Hey, young lady, just what do you think you are trying to do to a poor old fisherman?'

Cassidy glanced up at the Chief's gentle protest. The tall fisherman was holding one hand before his eyes to protect them from the glare coming from the powder-compact mirror held in Arlena's hands.

'Sorry, Chiefy.' She smiled, then turned her head to stare directly at Cassidy. 'Jimmy gave me this,' she stated simply, and he knew that the moment he feared had come. She was ready to talk about it, and as always, talked with disarming directness as she gazed at the river. 'It was all over next to nothing, Abe, father outlawing Jimmy, I mean. He thought I was in love with him, as did almost everyone, except myself and Jimmy, that is . . .'

Cassidy blinked. Was he hearing right? She met his gaze.

'What we both loved was the county and its people,' she continued. 'I half suspected that deep down Jimmy might love me. But I know he loved this place more. It was everything to him, and we both hated what father was doing to it. I was quite ready to leave home in disgust but Jimmy persuaded me to stay on and help control father in any small way I might.' She smiled warmly. 'He was always recruiting people for the good fight . . . the way he did you boys.'

'How's that?'

Arlena rose and brushed down her plain quaker cloth skirt as she gazed over the river at the hills.

'Jimmy has an instinct for people. Somehow he must have sensed from the very start that you were like him and deserved to be helped any way he could. . . .' Her face clouded as he rose to stand beside her. 'Almost as though he needed to know there was someone here who would stand against father and care about the people, as you have proven you would.'

Cassidy's face showed thoughtful in the light bouncing off the pewter surface of the river. That would explain a lot, he thought. But there was something on his mind even weightier than Kaine and his disappearance directly following the Pawnee showdown. Something he must know.

'Arlena, it's likely the wrong time for this . . . but about you and me. . . .'

Live a hundred years, he would never forget the way her gray eyes looked when she said, almost shyly, 'Oh, I'm in love with you if that's what you mean, Abel Cassidy. I was from the first day I saw you. I'm like Jimmy in that way too. He knew you were his friend from that first day at the river, and from our first day, I knew you could be much more than that to me. I know in a strange way that Jimmy wanted us to have one another. In fact I'm quite certain he was waiting for me to find a man like you to look after me before he could leave . . . I hope that you feel . . .'

Her words were cut off by his mouth against hers. The Chief smiled even though nothing was biting. There was only one thing that could round off his happiness. But nobody had heard or seen anything of Jimmy in three long days.

They were tired at the end of a hard day and coffee tasted just fine as they sat on the stoop watching daylight draining from the sky above the hills. Visitors and well-wishers and officials from the commissioner's office had been welcomed by Goober's booming bark through all their many comings and goings over recent days, yet the trail hound seemed totally unaware of the rider on the black-tailed mustang until he reined in before the cabin.

It was Kaine!

He was slender and lean in the familiar range clothes of a working cowhand with two big Colt revolvers slung across slim hips. He looked the same as before, from a distance. But as they crossed to him they realized there was a chilling difference. His air of casual authority was still evident, but the youthful face was gaunt and white and they now saw that layers of stained strapping encircled his slender waist. There was a hint of sternness in the set of the young face, a formidable directness in the look he put upon them as his mustang stamped a foot and whiffled impatiently.

'Evenin', cowmen.' He winced as he fingered his hat back and gazed around. 'Mighty peaceful hereabouts tonight . . .' He glanced upwards and seemed to be drinking in everything, the dark of the hills outlined against the daylight burning away over Mount Ratenal like an old fire, as though storing them away in his memory. 'Well, you've had yourselves a busy time recently and you've sure earned your rest, so I'll be moseyin'.'

All three began speaking at once but the young rider seemed not to hear. Momentarily his eyes met Cassidy's and what passed between them was something the latter seemed to completely understand, a look that told him the restless young drifter was easy at last. The hoofbeats faded into the darkness. It was Luke who said what each man felt:

'Y'know, I got a powerful feelin' we're not goin' to see him again.' And he was right.

A miner came across the body a week later. The man found him seated as though sleeping at the base of an ironstone cliff below Mount Ratenal which commanded a panoramic view that stretched for miles, his loyal mustang half-starved by his side. The funeral was the largest in the history of Buffalo County.

'So, just what did you expect to see?' Cassidy demanded.

Saddle leather creaked in the heat as they stared across

at the plain pine marker bearing the name; JAMES JUSTIN KAINE. The grave was exactly as they'd seen it last here in his chosen ground. Simple, dignified, well tended. Jimmy the Boy was still obviously sleeping undisturbed here through eternity with, amongst others, a brush salesman, a mother of five taken by the cholera and a young bronc-stomper who, according to his sad inscription, had died of a broken heart.

Nothing was different, yet somehow Pike and Waco appeared disappointed as the latter tugged the clipping from the pocket of his cowboy shirt.

'But this claims Kaine was sighted fishin' with the Chief up by Conway's Falls at the weekend, Abe,' he insisted stubbornly. 'You say they were seein' things?'

'Sensible God-fearin' folk saw him, pard,' Pike affirmed stubbornly. He snatched the clipping from Waco and passed it to Cassidy. 'See for yourself.'

Cassidy merely glanced at the clipping. He'd read the piece just once, which of course was all it was worth. All it told him, was that legends could be unpredictable things. Legends had drawn them West, and they may have even created one or two of the modest variety themselves. Some legends were patently bogus while others stood up well to scrutiny. Jimmy the Boy's seemed set to flourish now that it was plainly making the transition from reality into living folklore. He was dead and gone. But some would always want it otherwise.

Which was how it should be, he mused. But they had a ranch to run.

'All right, let's dust,' he said briskly. 'You fiddle-foots dragged me out here today because you expected to find the grave empty and Jimmy off riding someplace, which means you've got more leisure time on your hands than is good for you. But we can sure cure that.' He glanced at the sun. 'We can be back in the top forty by two, and we will be.'

They wanted to argue. Ever since coming across that article it seemed Waco and Pike had been collecting stories that had Jimmy Kaine being sighted many times since his death, racing about the countryside, talking to folks about crops and hard times; one imaginative farmer even insisted he'd spent a whole day on his place helping him sink a well.

So they'd insisted on coming here today to the broken-down fence, the sickly sycamores and the young cedar which still didn't appear to be thriving in the grudging soil. But Cassidy was being of no help, while everything here seemed exactly as it had been before, normal and undisturbed. And though Pike and Waco seemed vaguely disappointed as they finally turned to go, at the same time Cassidy felt they were secretly relieved to find the man named Jimmy Kaine still here where they'd left him – just like the horsebreaker, the drummer and the mother of five.

The dust of their going settled softly over sycamores, cedar and graves. The cloudless sky was white with heat.

Time brought great change to the big country and those who called it home. By the turn of the century cities stood where lonesome cowboys had once cold-camped out on the range. There was a rich man with a horseless carriage up at Merion nowadays, and Buffalo County had learned not to be embarrassed by its richly tapestried yet often violent past, but rather to take great pride in it, to vaunt it for what it had been and how it had shaped them.

Nowhere is this change more evident than on Oakey

Hill. Today the surrounding fence is of gleaming white stucco and concrete, and a hard-topped road lined by stately oaks leads the visitor up to the wrought-iron gateway flanked by a gleaming brass plate which announces proudly;

FINAL RESTING PLACE
OF
JAMES JUSTIN KAINE

History has been kind to Jimmy the Boy. It has glossed over the shortcomings of a remarkable life lived out against a vivid backdrop of Indian wars, pitched battles between Good and Evil, incredible feats of bravery and foolhardiness and the many things he did for the Old West and its everyday people, a generous sense of mission which eventually cost his young life.

The cheap marker is long gone, in its place a gleaming obelisk of polished granite donated by the families of Abe and Arlena Cassidy and those of Waco and Pike of the vastly expanded Turtle Ranch and their many sons and grandsons.

The cedar is a giant now and the visitors who come to the hill experience mixed emotions, most of them charmed and impressed and a few less so. Yet one response is common, and this is an awareness of the almost palpable air of calm and tranquillity of the place experienced by virtually everybody who takes the time to sit on the big wooden benches beneath the mighty cedar, from the comfort of which they may study the gold-leafed inscription upon the burnished obelisk at their leisure.

Some attribute this unique atmosphere to the favorable location of Oakey Hill while others believe it stems naturally from the meticulously tended graveyard-grounds and landscaped surrounds.

A remarkable number however, having once sat here reliving a past they have only ever read about in books, or have had passed on by the storytellers, leave unshaken in their conviction that the profound sense of peace they experience and take away with them emanates from the very earth of this special place itself and the once wild boy who sleeps below.